9-26-2011

Susan ~

My Sister girl,

Love Joy

RETSIS

Bridget Davis

Enjoy ~ Bridget D

Murdock Publishing Company

Murdock Publishing Company
A Division of Black and White Enterprises

This is a work of fiction. The characters, incidents, and dialogues are products of the author's imagination and are not to be construed as real. Any resemblance to actual events or persons, living or dead, is entirely coincidental.

ISBN: 0-9668865-1-8

Printed in the United States of America

ACKNOWLEDGMENTS

To all of you who have been a part of my life.
I thank you, and I love you.

My children, Racquel and Kenny, I love you.
My husband, father and sisters, I love you.
I miss you mommy.

My Attorney, Pamela Crockett, Esq. you are phenomenal.

To My Editor, Helyn George, you are the best.

To all of my school teachers and to all of the nurses that
I have worked with, thank you for the enlightening
experiences throughout the years.

CHAPTER
ONE

It was twenty-five years ago to the day that Sister and I met. When I close my eyes to reminisce back to September 30, 1955, my entire life makes sense. My entire existence imminently usable; without a doubt, by the laws of man. My purpose for living was planned from the beginning of time. I was supposed to be here on earth.

September 30, 1955

The smell of the fresh autumn air was so thick that it could have been canned tight, to be opened and savored on a cold winter's night. The leaves were turning orange and had begun falling from the trees in slow motion, as if they were dancing to the whisper of a smooth tune.

This particular day had gotten off to a good start. However, there was just something unexplainably different. The scent in the air and the feeling of peace and serenity had encased our tiny apartment that my grandmother, GiGi, and I had shared for the last seven years. This day was different from any other day GiGi and I had experienced. GiGi maintained her same routine of the day: the usual washing clothes, ironing and then cleaning our small two bedroom apartment downtown on 23rd Street in Manhattan. Although the apartment was small, it was able to meet our needs as far as space was concerned. And most importantly, GiGi prayed in her little closet just as she did everyday that I could remember for the seven years of my life. This praying routine that grandmother had allocated so much of her time to was beyond my comprehension. I thought she wasted too much time of a valuable day in that closet. I needed to know why she was wasting so much time, and finally, I conjured up enough courage to ask. I needed to hear this in her own words.

"GiGi, how come you pray so much?" I asked in a small voice.

She answered with a big smile while giving me a hug, "Sweetie, it's my insurance policy that I have with the Lord to make sure that you stay safe, your children stay safe, and your children's children stay safe."

"Well how come momma didn't stay safe GiGi? You said that she died seven years ago. Didn't you have some of that insurance with the Lord on momma?" I said, as my inner curiosity added courage to my questions.

"Yes, Rachel, the Lord needed another angel to do some work for him right away so he had to take your momma when he did. Your momma was only eighteen years old when she passed away, Rachel. Oh, that was the worst day of my life." GiGi's face was changing with sadness right before my eyes. Her eyes began to fill with water, which stayed in the corners of her eyes without falling out as she continued to share momma's death with me. She said, "I thought I would lose my mind. I knew that I couldn't lose my mind because then there would be no one to look after you, Rachel. Your mother, Margaret, or should I say Monty, was an only child. You are an only child. Your father died right before the Korean War, and I have no sisters or brothers. My only sister died right after you were born. It's just you and me, Rachel."

I looked into GiGi's eyes. It was evident that her heart was broken but not her spirit. She continued to try and explain to me the rationale for Momma dying so suddenly.

"That's what you would call a temporary lapsed policy. Rachel, yes, her time was up. I guess nobody else could get the job done for the Almighty like your momma. That's why he saw fit to take her away from us so unexpectedly. He just rearranged the policy, Rachel. I know this is very difficult for you to understand; it is also difficult for me to understand, my little sweetie."

"GiGi , I really wish that he didn't have to take momma so soon. I can't believe that momma was the only person in the world that was able to get God's work done as an angel. Only if he could have given me a chance to meet her — to see her face, to touch her hands, to smell the scent of her skin. This might have given me a better understanding of why my eyes are dark brown, why my hair is curly, why I have dimples on both sides of my face with high cheek bones, and why the color of my skin is dark olive," I said.

"And why you are so special?" GiGi interrupted. "I miss your momma, Rachel, more than you will ever imagine. But sweetie, you've got to believe that she is with us everyday at all times. Your momma had brown curly hair and brown eyes. She also had pretty little dimples like yours." I looked at GiGi and gave her a big hug and a kiss.

GiGi, now focusing on the first question that I asked her, answered spontaneously without taking a verbal break from her description of momma's appearance.

"Rachel, that closet, there," she said pointing. "It is my secret place of the most high, and in my secret place in the closet, I am alone with the Lord. Just the two of us. There are no interruptions, and the spirit is strong. And that's where I'm fitting to go right now for about fifteen minutes. You go on downstairs and play out front of the building. I'll meet you outside in a little bit. Go on now before I change my mind." She motioned me with her hand to run along.

I watched GiGi walk toward her closet, turn on her little lamp that sat on the small table inside the closet. As GiGi walked into her closet and knelt down to pray, I could see that her body was tired. Her knees could take the pressure of kneeling, after all she was only sixty-five years old. I grabbed my pretty yellow sweater off of the hook, swung it over my shoulder, and skipped fast down the stairs. As I skipped down the stairs, I was singing my favorite song that I learned in church the previous Sunday, "This Little Light of Mine, I'm Gonna Let it Shine." Approaching the last level of the staircase, I could see a pretty large shiny red ball in the corner next to the wall of the main entrance, just inside the building.

"Where did this ball come from? Hmm," I said to myself. There were no other children around my age living in the apartment building or anywhere nearby that I was aware of. Anyway, I picked up the ball and continued to skip while singing to the top of my voice to the other side of the street while bouncing the ball. This was somewhat of a challenge for me to skip and bounce the ball at the same time. Just that quick, the ball rolled out of my hands and into the street; I stopped singing. At that exact same time, I stepped down off of the curb into the street to get the ball. I heard a small voice call out my name.

Rachel. Rachel. Rachel. My name floated like the wind.

And just as I turned to see who was calling my name, a car came out of nowhere traveling about 90 miles an hour after coming around the corner. If I hadn't stopped to turn around to see who was calling my name, I might have gotten hit by that speeding car and perhaps joined momma in heaven. My heart was pounding out of my chest with fear. Now I was truly happy GiGi had started that insurance policy with the Lord, and the policy included me.

I turned all the way around, and there stood a small girl about my age. Her skin was beautiful complexioned, olive-colored skin with deep-setting black eyes just like mine. This girl could not have been older than six or seven years old. Looking at this girl made me feel as if I were looking in the mirror. We were even the same exact height.

"Hey girl, how did you know my name?" I said.

The girl stood still with her arms folded across her chest.

"I didn't call you by your name, did I?" she said.

"Yes, you did. You said, 'Rachel,' and that is my name."

The girl smiled, not saying a word. She had the most beautiful white teeth that I had ever seen and the smoothest skin like velvet. I smiled back.

"Where do you live?" I asked thinking that she would say she didn't live in the neighborhood, and she was visiting relatives.

The girl unfolded one arm, stretched it out straight-ahead of her, and pointed ahead. "I live down there."

"Down where?" I said.

She pointed straight ahead again. I still didn't see any apartment buildings where she was pointing. All I could see were a few department stores, an old warehouse and a couple condemned buildings that were probably around before Gigi was born. GiGi always said that I should never be rude to anyone by asking the same question over and over, and to this girl, it would perhaps seem rude since she already answered my question. Therefore, I didn't ask again.

"Well anyway, I'm sure glad you moved into the neighborhood because there are no other children our age around here. It can get lonely after school when you want to play. The children around here are all teenagers. What is your name by the way?"

This pretty but strange girl spoke in a singing voice that was unique to any voice that I had ever heard. "My name is Sister," she said as she twisted her pony tail pulled to the front of her shoulder. Her hairstyle was just like mine.

"Sister? What kind of name is that? I mean what is your real name?" I said.

"I said, 'My name is Sister.' That is the name that my father gave me when I was born."

I looked at Sister smiled and said, "You have a nice name."

By this time, GiGi had finally made it out of her secret closet of prayer, resuming her position on the stoop in front of our apartment building in her portable rocking chair that she brought downstairs to sit on.

I went to reach for Sister's hand to escort her over to GiGi, and she pulled back her hand away from me. I guess I had invaded her comfort zone. That was fine with me; I didn't feel offended. My intentions were to introduce her to GiGi, and to show grandmother that there was another girl my age living in the neighborhood.

"Sister, come on and let me introduce you to GiGi. She is my grandmother." I began to skip across the street, and when I turned back around, Sister was gone. I thought that Sister was right behind me, following my every step. She wasn't.

GiGi looked at me as if I were crazy. She probably thought that I had been talking to myself or to an imaginary friend. I don't think that GiGi ever saw Sister because I was standing in front of her, blocking GiGi's direct view.

I began to tell GiGi about my new friend who I had just met. GiGi continued singing her church hymns while knitting my new pink sweater that was anticipated for completion for my eighth birthday in two weeks. Thinking to myself, I still didn't understand where Sister could have disappeared to so fast. What a strange encounter that was.

I skipped back across the street to get that pretty red ball that I had found, and it was also gone. I couldn't understand why Sister took off so fast and with my new red ball. Surely she must have known that the ball belonged to me, and that it wasn't hers.

The sky began to turn gray and the leaves no longer took their perfectly still places on the ground. The wind began to move fast with aggression, almost like an angry man coming through town to inflict discipline on the disobedient. As the rain poured from the sky, grandmother and I quickly ran inside of our apartment building to seek refuge from the uninvited storm.

We lived on the second floor; therefore, GiGi didn't have to walk up too many stairs to reach our apartment. Although GiGi was an older woman, she was a physically strong woman. She never went to the hospital and always had her own original recipes for healing any illness that had invaded our bodies, along with prayer. Between prayer and her special medicine silver-seal concoctions, she was able to rid our bodies of any viruses or bacteria that tried to take possession.

Grandmother played some music by Mahalia Jackson and sang along the entire songs through as she often did. She had a terrible singing voice. Her voice was raspy and deep, a cross between Louie

Armstrong and Dinah Washington. She sang while we changed into dry clothes. While GiGi continued to sing, I joined in while looking out of our front room window. My singing voice was no better. I just could not understand how Sister disappeared so fast; she didn't even have the courtesy to say good-bye. This bothered me. I wondered if I would ever be able to make friends. Why did I scare Sister off? I knew for sure that her momma didn't teach her any manners. To take off so abruptly was rude. Maybe I'll see her at church Sunday or in Sunday school.

Next Sunday is the Sunday that I get baptized in church. I haven't told Grandmother yet, but I am afraid to get pushed down under the water. Our minister is a strong big man, Pastor Neil. His voice is deep, and he doesn't tell you when to hold your nose before he dips you under in the pool that is up on the pulpit. The scary thing is that he keeps you under the water for a few minutes at a time.

Everyone in the church looks on while singing "Soon and Very Soon, We are Going To See the King." If you were drowning, no one would know because everyone in the church is too busy singing.

"Rachel," GiGi called out from the kitchen. "Go and wash your face and hands Supper is ready."

I ran into the bathroom, cleaned up, and rushed back to sit at the kitchen table. I couldn't wait to eat; I was starving. GiGi had prepared my favorite meal for supper: gumbo seafood soup and homemade biscuits. I was hoping that GiGi would shorten the dinner prayer this evening because I was so hungry. As it turned out, GiGi didn't shorten the prayer; as a matter of fact, I think that she prayed for an extra ten minutes. I was peeking with one eye opened as she prayed and wiped the sweat from her head away with her hanky. I managed to pick pieces of corn out from the bowl that sat in front of me, and I started eating before GiGi was finished praying.

When we were done eating, I washed all of the dishes in the sink and managed to neatly place all of the leftovers in the refrigerator without breaking any bowls. GiGi and I sat around talking after supper. We talked about the importance of always doing the right thing in life regardless of the consequences. When it was time to turn in for the night, GiGi read the Bible to me, as she did every night that I could remember. Her favorite Scriptures that she read to me over and over again were out of the book of Daniel, II Thessalonians, and last but not least the book of Revelations, Chapter 13 through 16. It was almost as if GiGi was driven by some unknown force to introduce me to Daniel and prepare me in advance for a war that only she anticipated. I didn't understand Revelations, all of the talk about the Beast and the Dragon, the Seven Angels with the Seven Plagues. Sometimes I would ask grandmother questions, and she would answer my questions the best that she could. Then I would fall off to sleep as she continued to read.

GiGi and I lived with this same routine for the next eight years. The one thing that did change was that I was now attending high school.

CHAPTER
TWO

I was fifteen years old and in the tenth grade. My life had taken a turn for the better. The many friends that I had accumulated had relieved my friendship worries from eight years ago. I knew that there was something about me that was different from the other girls my age who I went to school with, considering the way Sister had taken off had left me paranoid for the last eight years as to whether or not I could have friends. September 30, 1955, was the last time that I had seen Sister. I looked out of the window year after year to see her without success. I even went up the street where she said that she had lived and asked around for her. No one and I mean no one had any clue who I was talking about or looking for.

By this time GiGi was seventy-three years old and her health began to fail. She didn't get around as much or as fast. She used a cane for assistance while walking throughout the apartment, often complaining of body aches. I completed most of the cooking and cleaning in the apartment that we had shared for more than fifteen years. I had managed to perform quite well in school, maintaining a 4.0 average and being on the honor roll in school for the last four years. GiGi was proud of my academic achievements and so was I.

She often told me how proud she was of me being able to help around the house while continuing to excel in school academically and how much it all meant to her that I was a nice young lady.

Little did GiGi know was that she was my motivating factor for my every decision, my every choice. She was my source of strength. I loved her dearly. She was all that I had, and I had to make sure that I didn't lose her. Her entire head of hair had turned silver. Her little worn body began to lean forward when she walked. All of these factors of the aging process never stopped GiGi from entering into her little closet, her secret place of the most high. She continued to pray on her hands and knees every day without interruption.

Preparing for my sweet sixteenth birthday party was a job in itself. Deciding what invitations to purchase and what color decorations to choose was more challenging than I had anticipated. GiGi was excited. This was our first gathering at the apartment ever. I decided to pay for everything myself, for I had a part-time job at the school, working as a file clerk after school two hours a day, and I had been saving my money for this occasion. There were many friends to invite since I had become quite popular at school due to my academic achievements and had gotten to know many of the other students.

There was one girl in particular that I had befriended. Her name was Retsis. She was new to the school, not from this area of town. It was absolutely remarkable how much we had in common. We had become best friends. People mistook us for sisters, stating that we bore a remarkable resemblance. We would talk on the telephone for hours at a time, discussing chemistry and the correct formulas using the periodic table from our chemistry class. There was no doubt that academically she had me beat. I was no slouch; however, Retsis was brilliant.

Retsis was being raised solely by her father. She would often say that she was not allowed to visit much with anyone because her father was strict. Her father, for one reason or another, never allowed Retsis to visit at my apartment. These reasons were even unknown to her.

Retsis would often say that her father was a bit over protective because she was all that he had left. Her mother had died when she was a baby, just like my momma Monty died when I was a baby. I'm not quite sure how old Retsis was when her mother died or if she got the chance to know who her mother was. In the past, I had asked GiGi how my mother died, and she changed the subject. I guess she thought at the time that I was asking that I couldn't handle the truth. Actually, it was only four years ago that GiGi finally told me exactly how momma died. Momma had died while giving birth to me. I felt awful. I felt responsible and guilty for something that was completely out of my control. And it wasn't until recently, when I confided in Retsis and Pastor Neil concerning my guilt, I felt a lot better. The guilt that I began to harbor after finding out how momma passed away was gone. I realized for sure, without a doubt that I had no control over that situation.

As the days grew closer to my birthday and my sweet sixteen birthday party, Retsis was working hard to make sure the occasion would be a memorable one. Many times I asked her if she was the one who I had met briefly eight years ago. She looked at me as if I were crazy; however, she never gave me a straight answer. Although she doesn't look like the small girl Sister, she had that same calm character, something different about her that I couldn't put my finger on. Her demeanor and her tone of voice was absolutely unique to my experience of characters encountered up until that point in my life.

I felt a sense of complete peace while in her presence, and she seemed to have the answers to every difficult situation and question. Retsis had no other friends in the school. Many of the other girls thought that she was a bit odd. Different would best describe her. That was OK because I too was also different than the ordinary girls my age.

I decided to telephone Retsis to make some party plans over the telephone.

"Hello, may I speak with Retsis?"

"Speaking."

"Oh hi Retsis, this is Rachel."

"I know who this is." We both began laughing at the same time.

Retsis and I talked on the phone for about one hour, deciding on which boys to invite. I liked a boy named Shelton, and I think that Retsis liked a boy named Michael, although she would never admit to it when I would ask her. Anyway, if she did like Michael, I could not see what she saw in Michael. He was truly a nerd, a loner who never made eye contact with anyone. But the more I thought about this match between her and Michael, I realized that it would be perfect. With Michael being a nerd and having the only ability to recognize intelligence in a person, this would be a match made in heaven. Michael is the only boy who would be able to not notice Retsis' odd style of dressing. Her long colorful dresses without a hem at the bottom that sometimes took on the appearance of a choir robe. Her cat glasses were one of a kind, because of the two large butterflies at each end of her frames. Last but not least, Retsis would kneel down for prayer at any given time while at school. Even the teachers thought Retsis was odd. Although she was odd she had a special way of making people feel relaxed with her calm, soft spoken voice. We continued to discuss which boys would be invited and which boys wouldn't be invited and why.

The list of invited boys was up to seven and the list of girls was up to nine. This list was larger than anticipated, and Retsis and I would have to rearrange the living room furniture to accommodate the sixteen guests. GiGi had no problem with the crowd invited; she was just concerned with this party being perfect and clean. Clean meaning no cigarette smoking and no beer drinking.

I was allowed to only play a few selected songs in which the lyrics told a nice story. Of course, GiGi insisted on baking the cake. She said the thought of me buying a cake from the bakery was ridiculous and out of the question. Everything was coming along smoothly.

Retsis finally agreed to come over to the apartment to help with the planning of the party. We were just not making the same progress over the telephone as we would make in person.

"Rachel, I know every time in the past when I asked my father if I could visit with you at your apartment, he would always make excuses. We had a talk last night, Rachel, and he had finally let up with being so over protective. He has agreed to allow me to visit with you now," she said.

In the past Retsis had always made excuses why she was not able to come over. Her number one excuse for not coming to my apartment was that her father said, "No, not yet." I couldn't understand what he meant by that. I was beginning to think and feel that her and her father thought that GiGi and I wouldn't allow her to leave when she got ready to, that we would perhaps keep her in our apartment against her will.

"Retsis, what time do you think that you will make it over here?" I said.

"Well if I leave right now, I could get to your place in twenty minutes," she said.

"Sounds great. I cannot believe that you will finally get to meet my grandmother. In fifteen minutes I will go downstairs to wait for you to bring you upstairs."

"That isn't necessary, Rachel. Just tell me what apartment you live in, and I'll find it," she said. Retsis' voice had suddenly changed. I could hear a boisterous tone in her voice. Was I being a pest to her? I thought. Did she really not want to come over, visit and meet GiGi.

"OK, I really don't mind waiting for you downstairs; however, if you insist on me not meeting you downstairs then I won't."

There was a moment of silence on the phone and I ended the conversation by saying, "I'll see you in twenty minutes."

I hung up the telephone and ran to GiGi's room to tell her the good news about Retsis finally getting permission to come over to meet her, and GiGi wasn't in her bedroom. From where I was standing, I could see her little light on in her closet. I thought Hmm, GiGi is praying awfully long this evening. She usually prays for no longer than an hour in the afternoon. She had been in that closet since approximately four o' clock and it was now five forty-five. This meant that she had been in that closet for an extra forty-five minutes. This was not like her.

I placed my ear to the closed door of the closet to try and hear some type of activity going on. I couldn't hear anything. Nothing but silence. Should I knock on the door? I have never interrupted GiGi during her prayer sessions. Neither had she ever prayed this long. My mind was racing. I decided to knock softly on the door of her closet. With three soft taps, I knocked on the closet door.

"GiGi are you in there?" I asked softly. She didn't answer. Fear began to enter my body. Trying to remain calm, I knocked three more times on the closet door, this time knocking harder. Still no answer. I twisted the doorknob and opened the door. GiGi's small body was slumped over her little table that she used to rest her Bible on. How could she have fallen asleep in such an awkward position?

"Grandmother, wake up let me help you into your bed."

GiGi didn't move. She didn't answer me either.

I repeated louder, "GiGi wake up. Come on grandmother, you cannot sleep like this all night or you'll surely have a backache and a headache in the morning." As I proceeded to help GiGi to her feet her body felt cold, and I noticed her eyes were rolled back in her head.

I began screaming, "GiGi wake up. You are scaring me. Please, Grandmother. I'm afraid."

I pulled GiGi's small frail body toward me while cradling her head in my chest rocking back and forth on my knees. I could not entertain the thought that perhaps GiGi was gone. I tried feeling for a pulse at the inside of her wrist and couldn't feel anything. I placed my hand on the front of her chest to try and feel for her heart beating; I felt nothing.

This just couldn't be. She is the one who told me all of her prayers for all of those many many hours and many many years was the insurance policy for us. The policy with the direct link to longevity and safety validated by the most high. Could it be perhaps her policy had just lapsed?

I began crying and let out a scream that was so loud, "No." I then tried to feel for a pulse again on her neck, like I had seen on television. I put the side of my face to her nose to feel if she was breathing. Nothing, no pulse, and no breathing. I knew that GiGi was dead. I could not accept this fact. This meant that I had no one, no other living relatives that I knew of. What was I supposed to do now? I never cried so hard in my entire life.

I wanted to go back to yesterday morning when I saw GiGi walking out of the kitchen laughing at my hair sticking straight up on the top of my head after waking up from a sound sleep.

I got up off of the floor after gently placing GiGi's head on a small pillow on the floor that she had also kept in the closet to place her knees on while praying. There was no doubt at this point that she had passed on and had been dead for at least a half hour. As I stood to my feet and turned around, there stood Retsis. I looked at Retsis not asking her how she got into the apartment and began sobbing uncontrollably. Retsis hugged me tight and said in a whispered voice in my ear, "Rachel, she was ready. It was her time, she didn't have a choice she had to go."

I yelled out to the top of my voice. "She could have at least said good-bye to me." I felt light headed and weak.

"Come over here Rachel and sit down in this chair, " Retsis said.

Retsis put her arm around my shoulder as she stood beside the chair I was sitting in.

"Rachel, there are many circumstances and situations in life that we cannot change. We just do not have the power or the answers to do such. I know that you will miss GiGi but listen my friend, she will continue to walk with you through your life just as Monty has."

Chills began to run through my body. Retsis had suddenly taken on the appearance of a caring parent. Her take-charge attitude was something that I had only witnessed in adults. I knew at times she could become aggressive and domineering. However, this side of her I had never seen. I felt really strange and weird as if she had some supernatural insight to the blueprints of my soul. Without hesitation, I asked Retsis, "How did you know about Monty? Or who Monty was?" Retsis answered,

" I guess you must have mentioned her to me in conversation at some point in our passing,"

"I don't ever remember mentioning to you that my mother's name was Monty."

Retsis shrugged her shoulders and said, "Now I remember, my father knew your mother."

"No, I don't think that your father knew my mother. She died at the age of eighteen."

I looked at Retsis, thinking to myself that maybe I did mention to her that my mother's name was Monty. The pain that I was feeling was devastating. I couldn't and didn't have the strength to deal with anything else at this time. I wanted to awaken from this dreadful nightmare.

"Listen to me, Rachel. I am going to fix you a nice cup of hot tea and then call the paramedics to come and pick up your grandmother's body."

"Retsis, I need to spend a little more time with her first." I got up from the chair and walked to the closet, to GiGi's cool lifeless body. I sat on the floor next to her, put her head in my lap, and began to speak while rubbing my hands through her thick head of silver hair. Although GiGi could not hear me, I needed to say what I was about to say anyway.

"GiGi, I love you. I knew no other mother except for you. You were there always for me, the first face I ever remember seeing. Just you and I, for all of my birthdays, Christmases. You didn't have much, but I never knew just how little we had. You saw to that. I know that you loved me more than life. Your dedication and loyalty as a caretaker and a parent remained constant as my entire life with you has been consistent."

I sobbed uncontrollably as I fought to hold back the tears unsuccessfully. My voice cracking with grief, I continued, "My eighth birthday, that beautiful pink sweater you knitted for me. I still have it. What am I supposed to do without you? How am I supposed to take care of myself without you at sixteen years old? GiGi, where are you? Wherever you are right now I wish that I were with you. I am so lonely already; I have no one."

The tears rolling down my cheeks nonstop.

"You have me."

I turned around, and Retsis was standing in the doorway of the closet with a hot cup of tea in her hand. I put GiGi's head down gently on the pillow, stood to my feet and took the tea from Retsis as I walked into GiGi's bedroom, which was right outside the closet.

"There will be someone arriving soon, Rachel, to pick up your grandmother," she said.

No sooner than the words left Retsis' lips there was a knock at the door. I opened the door and the paramedics stepped inside with the medical examiner. Retsis took over. She began telling the paramedics exactly what happened. They proceeded into GiGi's bedroom and into her closet. It was confirmed that she had no pulse and that she wasn't breathing. Yes, she was dead.

All of the questions that the medical examiner had regarding GiGi's past medical history, I was unable to answer. I had no clue if she had any serious preexisting illnesses. While trying to supply the pertinent information needed, Retsis walked over to one of the paramedics and whispered something in his ear. The paramedic nodded his head, smiled at Retsis, and said, "OK fellas, let's rap things up here." Another man proceeded to help the paramedic. They then put GiGi's lifeless body on the stretcher and then covered her body with a white sheet.

"Where are you taking her?" I said.

The coroner said, "Down to the morgue at St. Peter's Hospital.

You can make the funeral arrangements and have the undertaker pick up the body from the morgue when they are ready." I did not know the first thing about making funeral arrangements. This entire situation terrified me.

Retsis said, "Rachel, don't worry. When my grandmother's sister died, I helped make all of the arrangements for my grandmother, indirectly. I wouldn't mind helping you make the arrangements for your grandmother."

I just looked at Retsis; she is a special person who just had all of the answers for everything at the right time.

As I watched the paramedics carry GiGi's body out of the apartment, Retsis looked at me and a strong feeling of peace came over me. I didn't understand what was happening to me, I should be kicking screaming and crying from grief. I felt so at ease without a worry in the world. After all, GiGi was leaving this apartment for the last time, and my feelings just didn't match the circumstances.

Everyone left the apartment except for Retsis. I had decided to go lie down in GiGi's bed. I had become exhausted all of a sudden. Truly at this point, I could not keep my eyes opened. I didn't want to appear rude by going to sleep while I had company, but I needed to be alone at this time.

"Retsis, why don't you go home and get some rest. Thank you for everything."

Retsis said, "Absolutely not, I will not go home. I will stay here with you tonight and try to sort things out for you or with you. Go ahead and go to sleep now, Rachel. You look exhausted. Did your grandmother have an insurance policy that you know about?"

I looked up at Retsis and smiled, "Yes, Retsis, she had an insurance policy for herself, and oh, don't let me forget, yes, she had a policy for me, too. An insurance policy that lapsed without any

forewarning or any notices regardless if you're all paid up or not ."
Retsis looked at me with the weirdest expression.

"Your're tired, Rachel. Please go lie down and try and get some
sleep. I'll just look around here through your grandmother's belongings to see what I can find."

I decided to take Retsis' advice to take a nap. The perfect sleeping place, in GiGi's bed. I took my shoes off and decided to nap
with my clothes on because I had planned on getting back up this
evening and sorting through GiGi's papers. There was such an inner peace that I felt as I began to doze off to sleep in Grandmother's
bed. I didn't even remember closing my eyes.

CHAPTER
THREE

In my sleep, I heard a man's voice; it was a deep powerful voice that seemed to shake the bedroom walls from the vibration of each word spoken.

"Fret not, my child. I will grant you such fruitful rewards. Let not your troubles blind you, for I have sent a mighty warrior for you to follow and gain strength from. You must begin to prepare yourself for the unthinkable. Never wither in faith, for I have chosen you."

I sat straight up in the bed. Was that a dream or was there someone really in this room with me speaking to me? I looked around the room there was no one else in the room. From where GiGi's bed was located in the apartment, I could see Retsis sitting at the kitchen table with some papers in her hand. I ran into the kitchen to tell

Retsis about the voice that I heard while sleeping. I wasn't sure if I was dreaming or not. The voice was audible.

Before I could say anything without even turning around Retsis said, "Rachel, sit down here. Look what I found in your grandmother's belongings."

I walked closer to the table.

Waving a piece of paper in the air with her hand she said, "The insurance policy. It must be worth at least one million dollars."

I said, "No way! My GiGi did not have that kind of money to afford such an extravagant policy. Let me see."

Retsis handed me the policy to read. After reading the first two pages, I realized that Retsis was right. The policy was worth one million dollars. Thinking to myself, how could this be? I was more confused now then ever.

We lived tight financially, how could she have afforded the monthly premiums for this amount of insurance? So many thoughts were going through my mind at this point. I said to Retsis, "There is something wrong."

Retsis said, "Rachel, don't ever question a gift. Just thank the Lord."

This evening had seemed different, strange. The lighting in the apartment had appeared dimmer than usual. The smell of air in the house was like a fresh lemony smell, and the colors in the print in the furniture looked deeper in colors. Nothing made sense anymore. Did I also die? I wondered.

Finally I got the opportunity to tell Retsis about my dream with the loud man's voice, but I couldn't remember what the voice had said. Retsis showed no emotions. I guess she must have thought that I was losing my mind due to the stress of just losing GiGi.

Looking at me straight in the eyes after I had finished attempting unsuccessfully to tell her about the dream, she said, "Rachel, I will telephone the funeral parlor tomorrow morning to make the funeral arrangements for your grandmother."

"How do you know which funeral parlor GiGi wanted to have handle her services?" I said.

Retsis said, "Because it says right here on this document that I found that was with the insurance policy." Retsis began to read the document to me, "In the event of my death, I would like to have the funeral parlor And He Wept to handle my body, and the funeral services opened to everyone at Covenant Baptist Church. Also, I would like for someone to read a verse from the book of Daniel. I am naming Pastor Neil as Power of Attorney over my granddaughter Rachel Legna."

My grandmother had never mentioned any of this to me. All of the many nights we sat awake talking not once did she ever utter any of this. I gave Retsis a hug and thanked her for everything.

"Retsis, I think that perhaps you should telephone your father to let him know what happened here tonight and to let him know that you will be staying over here to keep me company tonight. If it is OK with him,"

Retsis said, "Rachel, after your tucked in and sleeping, I'll call."

I looked at Retsis and told her that she was my best friend and that I didn't know what I would have done this evening if she had not come over to the apartment.

Retsis smiled and said, " You would have managed just fine."

Retsis had a smile that could light up a room. Beautiful white teeth and skin like olive velvet. Retsis was ready to turn in for the night. I could tell by the way she was yawning.

"Rachel, do you have a nighty that I can borrow?"

I found a pair of P.Js that could fit Retsis after rambling through my drawers for about five minutes. I smiled because Retsis was so conservative, and all I had were nighties from two and three years ago. Retsis went into the bathroom to change. When she came out of the bathroom I laughed because on the front of the nightgown there was a picture of Mother Goose. I laughed because she looked totally ridiculous. Retsis grabbed a blanket and a pillow off of my bed and decided that she would be more comfortable on the sofa. From the sofa, she had a perfect view of GiGi's bedroom, where I was sleeping.

I was so happy that I didn't have to stay in the apartment alone tonight. GiGi's bed was comfortable, and I could still smell her body scent on her sheets, which for me kept her alive. I yelled out to Retsis, "Good night."

The next day, I was embarrassed, embarrassed because I had slept late into the afternoon. The large clock above the stove that I could see from GiGi's bedroom said that it was 2 p.m. How could I have slept for so many hours considering the responsibilities ahead me and considering the trauma of losing GiGi yesterday? Why didn't Retsis awaken me? The apartment was extremely quiet and dark. I jumped out of bed, put my bathrobe on, and went into the kitchen where Retsis was sitting at the table with her arms folded in front of her.

"Why didn't you awaken me?" I said.

"Well, you had a terrible evening last night, and I knew that your body needed the rest."

"Yes, my body needed the rest, but I have a busy day ahead of me today with much to accomplish."

Retsis said, "I made all of the arrangements as your grandmother requested, Rachel. I just got off of the telephone with my father and he wants me to stay here with you again tonight. My father wanted to know if he should come over right away, and I told him that everything had been taken care of already as far as the arrangements were concerned and that there was nothing that he could do here."

"Retsis, you should have let him come over; I would love to meet him."

Retsis looked at me and smiled.

" Retsis, you said that you made the funeral arrangements. When is the funeral scheduled?"

"Thursday at 10 a.m. Pastor Neil from your grandmother's church said that Thursday would be the best day for the church members of Covenant Baptist Church."

"Oh No! That is my birthday."

Retsis said, "Oh my, that's right. Well, we will change the date to Friday."

I said, "No, don't change it. There will be no sweet-sixteen-birthday party. I will telephone everyone letting them know that the party has been cancelled. I will also make sure that information on GiGi's funeral arrangements is placed in the newspaper under the obituary section just in case GiGi did have family members that I didn't know about."

CHAPTER
FOUR

The day of the funeral came quickly. Retsis stayed over at my apartment the night before so that we could leave to go to the funeral in the morning together. I had picked up a beautiful black dress from Macy's, and Retsis picked out the same identical dress to wear. When Retsis put the dress on, it were as if I was looking at myself. This was the worst birthday of my life. I had to now try and find a way to go on with my life without the direction, guidance, and love that I was so use to receiving from GiGi on a daily basis.

The funeral service was beautiful. Pastor Neil preached a sermon on Lazarus raising from the dead. Retsis really enjoyed the sermon. I could tell by her smile, which radiated across the entire church. Again, I began to feel that sense of peace that I had felt the night GiGi died. There was also a feeling of a presence nearby that

I couldn't describe. The best description would be of something out of the ordinary, supernatural. The entire church was filled with people. Some new; some I had never seen before.

There was one man who I noticed when I entered into the church who stood out. He was a handsome man, with structured features, high cheekbones, dark brown eyes. His hair was gray at the temples. Although he was sitting down, I could tell that he was a tall man by the length of his body torso and legs. This man was dressed well; however, the style of his suit was one from the past. It reminded me of old black and white pictures that I had seen once in a magazine. His black suit with a mandarin collar up against his white skin gave him an appearance of someone who was perhaps risen from the dead. I tried not to stare at him, but it was hard not to stare. His features were distinct. His skin was as white as a ghost.

After the service, I got the opportunity to meet a few of GiGi's friends who she grew up with in Brooklyn. The offers that I received from two of her close friends she went to school with were kind.

The offer to live in a different state with Stella, her friend was considerably tempting, and the offer to reside in Jamaica with her friend Wilomina of sixty years was more tempting. However, I had to decline all two offers. The road ahead that I anticipated was truly to be a scary one, but leaving my community and school at this time would make this experience that much more unbearable. I needed to remain in familiar territory. Pastor Neil assured me that my lifestyle would not change.

The days, the weeks went by fast without incident. The reality of GiGi's passing had settled in, and my life's routine was picked up from where I had left off.

I remained in the apartment without any hassles from the authorities. Thank goodness GiGi had provided legal clarification in her will that in the event of her death, I was to remain in the apartment under the guidance of Pastor Neil. GiGi had provided enough documentation in her will proving that I was responsible and requested I be declared an emancipated minor.

Retsis and I remained friends throughout the years. We both graduated from high school with honors, along with Michael who had also become a close friend of ours. Although I never met Retsis' father or any members of her family, I didn't find odd because they all moved south after GiGi passed away. Ironically the authority's never bothered Retsis for living alone as a minor. She survived off of money her dad would send monthly. Going south was not an option for Retsis.

Retsis decided to remain up north to attend Yale University. That choice was excellent. I was also accepted into Yale University with a full scholarship to study biochemistry.

I lived off of GiGi's insurance policy and continued to obey her rules of the house even after she had passed away. Then it was time for me to move on and leave the tiny two-bedroom apartment that I shared with GiGi for almost sixteen years of my life. This meant breaking all ties with what was familiar to me in my environment. Unfortunately, I had no choice. The commute to Yale would have been almost impossible on a daily basis, traveling from Manhattan to Connecticut.

Living in New Haven, Connecticut, could not be all that bad. Retsis, Michael, and I had to decide whether or not we would live on campus or share an apartment for four years. I was sure Retsis would know what was best for us she always did, I reasoned.

At the age of 18 years old, I was now ready to meet the challenge of an extended education head on. There was a purpose for my being as Retsis had often said; everyone had a mission, a challenge in life. To find that challenge in life and accomplish that mission was not in clear view as of yet. I didn't know what direction to focus clearly on in life, the momentum of desires never withering. My motivation, like a burning inferno, was the best way to describe the feelings from the inside of my body out. My mind constantly raced, wondering where my life would be in the next ten years. Would I be married? Have a decent paying job? And would I one day have children?

Where were these feelings coming from? I awakened in the morning with these feelings and went to sleep at night with the thoughts of one day, just running with the entire universe on my back to the finish line. Where was this finish line? This is what I had to find out.

Since GiGi passed away two years ago, I never heard that voice that I had heard in her bedroom the day she died. The voice had come and gone just as everything else in my life, except for Retsis. I had truly hoped that the voice would give me some sort of direction as to where my life was supposed to go.

Not even Retsis could help me with the answers to that question as smart as she was. Retsis was definitely an odd girl. Extremely intelligent with no limits to her academic boundaries, she had a take on every topic mentionable, including reincarnation in which was her favorite. Quiet with a peculiar sense of humor, she often handled herself with much grace. She remained a close friend with Michael, who continued to maintain an I.Q. of above 130. He had decided to follow Retsis and attend Yale. Michael no longer looked like the nerd he was in high school, but he took on the appearance of a modern, taller slimmer version of Einstein. I wouldn't describe him as handsome but the best description, distinguished and sexy looking with the potential to model for *The Elite Magazine of America.*

After class one evening, while getting acclamated to our environment at Yale, the three of us decided to scope the campus for a coffee shop. We stumbled upon a fast food place called Maximillion's and decided to stop in for a snack and check out the place. I thought this was a great idea. This would allow me to find out more about Michael's personal life. He was secretive and never discussed an attraction to anyone of the opposite sex. It was clear that he was interested only in his education. Although I had no physical attraction to him, I couldn't understand why the ladies were not knocking down his door. This was the perfect opportunity for questions.

We were hungry and ordered sandwiches and soda pop. While waiting for the sandwiches to be made I initiated the conversation.

"Michael, how do you like your room here at Yale? Is it comfortable enough for you?" I said.

"As comfortable as could be expected," he said.

"What do you think about your classes?" I said.

"They are a challenge. Just as life and everything that evolves around us," he said.

"Have you met or seen anyone that you might be interested in on a intimate level?" I said.

"Unfortunately, you inquisitive queen, I haven't. I am a man of priorities and time management is high on my list. It would be virtually impossible for me to seek out something so worldly at this point in my life," he said, giving me the most beautiful angelic smile that I had ever seen.

"I think Michael is wise to put his studies first, Rachel. Why attend Yale to find a mate? If that's what he was looking for, he could have stayed home for that." Retsis said.

"Well, you are both right again," I said, sarcastically while smiling.

We finished our sandwiches and drinks and turned in for the evening. That was the last conversation that I had with Michael regarding his personal life.

Retsis truly adored him, and it was obvious when in his presence her best qualities surfaced without her awareness. When he was around, she spoke differently, choosing her words carefully. Her body postures and gestures when speaking were perfect, flawless. Retsis absolutely radiated when Michael stepped into the room.

When I would ask Retsis if she was in love with Michael, she would respond, "I love everyone; I am in love with the beauty of the world and its greatest potential." She is only fooling herself I thought. I would smile at her and shake my head slowly to let her know that my suspicions of her love for Michael was accurate, and yes, she was oblivious with it. She let the cat out of the bag the evening the three of us had sandwiches at Maximillion's

Michael was happy attending Yale also. He often said that attending Yale University was a dream come true for him. He had no problems along with Retsis obtaining a scholarship to this Ivy League University. I was the one out of the three of us who had to stay awake around the clock more often than few, studying for the SATs and maintaining a 4.0 average in high school after GiGi's passing. Where I got the strength from I'll never know.

Often in the past, I heard GiGi say, "We never know how strong we are until we are put to the test." How could she have been right about so many things? I regret the fact that she never got the opportunity to meet Retsis or to attend my graduation from high school. That would have made life easier for me. Just to have gotten her opinion on Retsis, to have looked into her eyes as my name was called over and over to receive awards at the graduation ceremony. GiGi was always intuitive when it came to a person's character. Although deep down inside, I knew that Retsis was on the up and up, and GiGi would have loved her.

She was my best friend for almost three years, and I felt as if I had known her my entire life. Her mannerisms and gestures were identical to mine. The phrase "water seeks its own level" couldn't apply better to the both of us. We had the same taste in music. Her taste in clothes was a bit odd, but I liked them. We must have been sisters in our past lives.

I knew that the three of us would have a lifetime friendship. In the back of my mind, I knew that we would never be apart from one another. Our decision to attend the same university was definitely no coincidence. The three of us had a lot to get use to here at Yale. And we were helping each other adjust. Still unclear about what profession I wanted to obtain. I knew that I wanted to do something that would make a difference in someone's life. When GiGi died, I felt helpless. There was nothing that I could have done to save her life. If I became a doctor I could save the lives of many people. I was not obliged to devote all of my years here at Yale to science. A biochemist would allow me the same gratification of helping to save lives. After pondering for days, prior to my admission here at Yale, my intended major was biology and chemistry with the goal of becoming a biochemist. I was hoping that I didn't bite off more than I could chew. Retsis decided to major in theology. Why she chose such a difficult major, theology, I'll never know. Her dream just as Michael's, was to become a minister. I would probably work for a pharmaceutical company.

Retsis and Michael planned to fill out applications for employment. I had decided not to work my first semester, rather acclimating myself as much as I could to my new environment. With the task of cleaning out the apartment in New York that I had not completed prior to starting school, I dreaded the day coming that had finally arrived.

Michael and Retsis had volunteered to help me pack up all of my valuables in my apartment in New York. It took us all of two weeks to complete the task. I finally got everything out of the apartment, putting all of my possessions along with GiGi's possessions into storage. I was keeping everything; I had decided that nothing would be trashed.

In the process of putting our belongings into storage, I felt as if I were putting the memories of the past eighteen years of my life into storage. This process of putting GiGi's belongings into storage helped me to gain a better vision to where I was headed. Packing the stuff away finalized the past for me allowing me clearer insight to the future.

I was ready emotionally and spiritually to embrace the beginning of a new stage of my life and embellish what GiGi had already established in her investment in the building of a strong foundation of character within my existence. The visionary process that began, I believe, at my conception was imminently in GiGi's sight and vaguely in my sight.

Given not the fairest chances in life through my eyes regardless, I had to make life work. The pressure of the thought of failing became too difficult to ascertain. I knew that I was facing a challenging road ahead, but I truly had not a clue of why I so strongly felt this way. Could it have been perhaps I wasn't right at GiGi's side when she died? I often felt that if I had closely observed her that day, maybe I could have prevented her death. Forced into independence, I had to take on another task of college.

CHAPTER
FIVE

Yale was absolutely beautiful. The old campus was huge. I felt as if I were living in a kingdom from biblical time as I walked through the halls of the buildings. I imagined myself as being a Queen with a powerful hierarchy to rule. Yale had a magnificent atmosphere and was surrounded by people from all walks of life. As I strolled from one building to the next, the tall intricately carved brick buildings of tanish color reminded me of castles. The grassy areas were mowed, and the students picnicked for short breaks between classes. I loved it here.

Everything fell into place for me while attending Yale. The transition from high school to this prestigious university went as smoothly as one could ask for. The first year, I studied constantly. It paid off because my G.P.A. score was 4.0, and I was proud of my accomplishment. I had learned more in one year at Yale than I learned in my entire life. I was beginning to feel intelligent. My potential was limitless, and there was no stopping me now. Completing my pre requisite classes during my first year was a relief.

My second year at the university was a bit more of a challenge because the professors expected more. That was fine with me. The greater the challenge, the more exciting my life became. I was still happy after attending this university for two years.

Two years flew by at Yale. The first semester trying to get used to such a different lifestyle took a lot of adjustments for me. Surely money wasn't a problem for me with the extravagant and generous policy that GiGi had invested; the money for me would be around for the remaining of my life, if I spent wisely. I hadn't the foggiest idea of where Retsis and Michael's finances were coming from. Surely the fast food restaurant where they worked on campus wasn't pro-viding enough money to carry them through the long haul of their extended education here. Sure the three of us had scholarships, but it just touched the tip of the iceberg.

I often offered to lend Retsis and Michael a few dollars to make ends meet, but they repeatedly declined. I knew if I offered to give them money that would have been out of the question for them. I couldn't understand why.

Two more years remaining here at Yale, and I was convinced that I would find my prince charming at this palace of an Ivy League University. I had been feeling lonely, longing for a male compan-ion. The thought of spending the rest of my life without a male companion frightened me, for I eventually wanted a family with children and everything that went along with it. Most of the girls attending college here had boyfriends. What better place to find a prince charming other than at Yale? Now that I had mastered the academics, I could possibly have a personal life.

The loneliness within my soul consumed my thoughts. The sight of couples holding hands while walking on campus in the spring and fall had exacerbated the desire to be loved.

Reflecting back to four years ago on the voice that I heard the night GiGi died, I knew that had something to do with the outcome of my life. Suddenly I remembered the exact words spoken to me the night GiGi passed away, as if the person who spoke the words had restated them in my ear as a reminder.

"Fret not, my child. I will grant you such fruitful rewards. Let not your troubles blind you. For I have sent a mighty warrior for you to follow and gain strength from."

Up until this point, I had not thought about a serious relationship with anyone. There was now a burning desire for me to meet this warrior that the voice had spoke of. I am twenty years old and still a virgin. What is wrong with me? I often would ask myself. All of the young ladies on campus had male friends, and they were indulging in sex. Not Retsis, her and I were in the same club. The Man Free Club. Retsis continued to deny her feelings for Michael. And I had not seen Michael with any females.

There was a young man in my chemistry class who showed an interest in me. Was this the warrior? His appearance was flawless, and his intelligence was ingenuous. His structured face with deep-set gray eyes, he could have been mistaken for an archangel from heaven perhaps. His deep voice, his broad shoulders, and narrow hips held me captive for the one hour and ten minutes that I shared the space beside him in our chemistry class. Too shy to initiate a conversation with him, he would often make eye contact with me and smile.

The dimples that so perfectly increased with his smile took me to a place of serenity in which I had no desire to return to chemistry class or depart from that place in which he had taken me.

This chemistry class had truly stirred up some chemistry that was not on the periodic table that we so intensely studied. Those other chemical components that I felt were only identifiable to me, felt excellent. Now all I had to do was to attract his attention without making a fool of myself. This would take some ingenious thinking and maneuvering on my behalf because GiGi always told me that the first impression of a person was everlasting. The person to help me with this mission would be the person who always had a logical solution to everything—Retsis.

I couldn't wait to see Retsis to talk to her about this young man in my chemistry class. As soon as I got out of my English class, I ran over to meet Retsis at her next class which was two doors down from where my classroom was located. I ran right in to her.

"Retsis, I must talk to you, come over here and sit with me until the next class begins. There is this young man in my chemistry class who is intelligent and extremely handsome. I am totally physically attracted to him. His name is Natasto, and he brings out feelings in me that I cannot explain or submerge. Feelings that I have never felt before. The feelings are almost uncontrollable. I have never felt so out of control in my entire life. I am still a virgin at the age of 20, which has taken much discipline and control on my part thus far. Why am I feeling so out of control with these feelings and thoughts right now? If this is what lust is all about, I love the way it feels. However, I don't like the lack of control that accompanies it."

I was rambling on, and finally Retsis said, "Yes, I already know you're a virgin and so am I. Whats the big deal? Rachel, what do you know about this man? Where did he come from? These are the questions that you need to first ask yourself. Is it his charismatic demeanor that you feel so vulnerable to? Or is it what you don't know about him that you are attracted to?"

"I told you, Retsis, it was his appearance. His physical appearance that is. I know nothing about him except that he is studying to become a physician of nuclear medicine. His name is Natasto and that perhaps he may also be a genius. He looks almost as if he could have been born of an interracial conception or has some close Arabian descendants. He is gorgeous."

Retsis looked at me with the most peculiar look. A look of surprise would best describe her expression. I couldn't help but ask, "Why? Do you know this young man?"

Retsis responded, "No! The man that I know named Natasto is not as handsome as you are describing to me. Perhaps Michael may know who he is. I will see Michael later on today, and I will ask."

Retsis made everything so formal when she felt it to be important. She wanted to provide answers, giving me choices to choose from by using common sense. This behavior made me feel like she was testing my logic. We were the same age, there was no need for her to take on the big sister role. Truthfully I didn't consider this an issue.

"For now Rachel, my advice to you is don't you initiate anything. No conversation; no dates. Allow him to have the honor of making the first move. You must never lose control or power over any part of yourself. Don't let down your guards. Use your discernment that God has given you. Use your intuition. Use it always without determent of the different facets that may strike your fancy in the flesh. Let not your heart be taken, Rachel, by the cheap, gift-wrapped gifts of disaster. Nor let your soul be carried away by the army of destruction."

"Retsis, you're scaring me. Why are you talking like this? This doesn't sound like you; you sound like someone is speaking through you. I can hear your voice, but I know these are not your words."

Retsis gave me that look again, and then smiled and said, "Let the words of my mouth and the meditation of my heart be acceptable in thy sight. Now Rachel, those aren't my words. Those are the words from my father."

"Retsis, I didn't know that your father was a religious man."

Retsis smiled at me and said, "Rachel, my father is religious."

I always knew that Retsis and Michael had strong faith in God, and that they prayed as much as GiGi did. But I never realized just how spiritual they were. I should have realized. Who else would have the desire to study theology at eighteen years old? I knew deep down inside that Retsis would never ever give me bad advice, but I needed something more tangible to relate to.

I think that it was already too late for me to remain in control and not to lose power over any part of myself. I had already lost that battle. There was no control when it came to Natasto. He had already taken my heart. And yes, I had a burning desire to sleep with him. Some how I knew that if I did that, I would never recover and that he would have me hooked forever. My mind was telling me to squelch this desire and replace it with the challenge of maintaining a 4.0 average. That burden was too difficult to capture at this point.

I thought about Natasto with every waking moment. I dreamed about Natasto while sleeping. Dreaming that while with him in a small crampy space, I was completely submissive to him. In the dream I felt like a slave. I couldn't remember all of the details of this particular dream. What I had remembered was not impressive. This man had put a spell on me that could not be broken. I couldn't wait to get to class everyday.

I dressed from head to toe, wearing my best. I never liked makeup; instead, I purchased a facial moisturizing cream to soften my skin. With a little lip gloss applied to my lips, I felt as sexy as the next girl did who was wearing the eyeliner and red lipstick.

Finally, I conjured up enough nerve and courage to ask Natasto to join me after school for a hot chocolate drink at the campus store. "I would be honored to join you, Rachel, for a warm drink at the campus store," he said.

I could not detect any emotion in his voice. He was straight forward and to the point. More of the conservative type and probably full of surprises which really left me wondering what was in store for the future if there was to be one.

CHAPTER
SIX

I was beside myself with delight. Anxiety ridden and just totally over the edge of the world with happiness. I knew that I had to get back to my dorm, change clothes, and freshen up. My stomach felt nervous, and I could not bear waiting three more hours just to spend about two hours at the most with Natasto. How long could it take to sip on a cup of hot chocolate?

Natasto and I both agreed to meet at Maximillion's at 6 p.m. I decided to arrive about ten minutes early to find Michael and Retsis working behind the serving counter. This was their day off, and I was surprised to see them there. I explained to Michael and Retsis that I was to meet Nataso for a warm drink shortly. I got no reaction from either one of them. Looking through the glass window of the campus store, I could see Natasto from a distance approaching

Maximillion's. As he entered through the doorway, I could sense that something was wrong. I motioned him with my hand to come over to where I was sitting. I was excited.

Michael and Retsis approached the table we were sitting at after Natasto sat down. Natasto began to behave quite oddly. Moving around in his seat, it was obvious that he was uncomfortable. This was the best time I thought for me to introduce Natasto to Retsis and Michael.

"Retsis and Michael this is Natasto," I said.

Natasto could not keep still at this point. He was moving around in his chair as if ants were in his pants. I was extremely concerned and a bit embarrassed for him. At this point Michael and Retsis began their own conversation. What freaked me out was that their conversation wasn't in English. The two of them were speaking in several different languages. I could not understand any of it. Nataso got up to leave but not before he yelled out some words in what sounded like a mixture of Hebrew and Italian. This situation was totally weird. As far as I knew Michael or Retsis never told me that they had taken any foreign languages in school or at any other place. And they had both never given me a straight answer when I had asked if they knew who Natasto was.

I truly did not know what to make of all of this. I looked at Retsis and Michael. They looked at me. Without further hesitation, Michael said, "Retsis and I had to complete two foreign languages as apart of our major in theology here at Yale."

Why couldn't you and Retsis just speak to Natasto in English?" I said.

Michael looked at Retsis hoping that she would respond to this question. Retsis calmly said, "Rachel, yes we could have spoken in English, but as apart of our study program, it was highly recommended by professor Daniel that we practice speaking Italian as often as we could."

"I just think that it is quite odd, Retsis, that you and Michael have never practiced speaking Italian around me before today. It's odd that you had to wait and speak this language when Natasto was around. I need to know what was said between the three of you, and I need to know now."

Michael looked at Retsis and said, "Please allow me to answer that question Retsis." Retsis looked at Michael and smiled.

"Rachel, I have shared a couple of classes with Natasto, and Retsis and I have had some dealings with him in the past that haven't been pleasant. Retsis and I didn't want to upset you when we learned of your attraction to this man."

"Upset me? I thought that we were friends. I thought that we had a relationship based on honesty and trust, and that there were no secrets when it came to the best interest of our lives."

Michael looked me in the eyes with a dead lock grip and said, "We were looking out for your best interest Rachel, and Retsis and I are your best friends. Our relationship with you cannot get any more honest then it is right now. Our main objective is to protect you."

"Protect me from what? The experience of having a meaningful relationship with a man that I am attracted to and possibly feeling loved by the opposite sex for once in my life?"

Michael responded with his voice slightly increasing in volume while Retsis looked on with an expression of sorrow. " If you must know we are trying to prevent you from dancing and sleeping with the devil."

I could feel the heat boiling under my skin as I felt myself becoming angry.

"How dare you? How dare you, Michael, think that you are

holier than thou? I always looked at you as being a man of sub-
stance and of high quality. Judgmental and opinionated is not what
I would have narrowed your character down to. This tunnel vision
that you have taken on so eloquently has depreciated your character, Michael. I see your new attitude as obscene, and I would strongly
suggest you take off that noble robe and join the rest of us here on
campus at Yale with our walk through life as students for the next
two years."

Retsis looked on not saying a word as I got up from the round
table where I was sitting and walked out. Retsis attempted to follow
me and I heard Michael say, "Let her go, Retsis. She needs time
alone time to think."

I walked for hours around the campus, hoping to bump into
Natasto. I knew that he lived on campus; however, I hadn't a clue to
which dorm he lived in. Michael and Retsis still had not told me
what they said to Natasto or what he had said to them. I just couldn't
wait to get to chemistry class tomorrow to ask him what went on at
Maximillion's.

After walking for three hours around the campus trying to make
sense of this evening, I decided that I was getting nowhere with
trying to rationalize the event that took place earlier. I was so angry;
the thought of Michael's new attitude boiled inside me. How dare
he say he was preventing me from dancing and sleeping with the
devil. What a mean gesture, I thought.

Just as I approached the entrance to my dormitory, I could see
Michael appear in the doorway. Before I could say anything Michael
said, "Rachel, I will tell you exactly what I said to Natasto verbatim;
however, you must promise me that you will not interrupt me until
I am finished speaking. You will not understand anything, Rachel,

that I am about to say to you, and that is OK What you must understand is that I am on a mission that is in your best interest. It is a mission that has been delegated by my father many years ago that must and will be carried out."

I said, "Michael, let's go upstairs and talk, here in the hallway is not an appropriate place for us to have such an intense conversation."

Michael nodded his head in agreement.

I was bubbling over with curiosity. On my way up to my room, I promised myself that I would keep an open mind to what Michael had to say.

As soon as we entered the tiny room, Michael began mumbling under his breath while using both of his hands to outline the sign of the cross. I couldn't understand or make out much of what he was saying except for "The angel sang, like voices from heaven in which no man has heard."

I had heard GiGi utter this same prayer many times in the past. Continuing to keep an opened mind I asked Michael,"What are you saying?"

"Rachel I am just repeating a verse that I memorized from my father. Michael looked around the room as if he felt the presence of someone else with us.

"Rachel, you asked me a question earlier in which I evaded the answer to. I am here now to repeat to you what I said to Natasto back at Maximillion's earlier this evening."

Michael pulled out the chair that I had under my desk, motioning me with his hand for me to sit down. I sat in the chair while Michael remained standing. He appeared calm with his arms folded in front of his chest, and looked directly at me. He began to speak.

"And there are hidden catastophies of this world. Without any understanding of the nucleus by man from whence he came. It is there in which he will return."

I continued to sit quietly while Michael spoke. None of what he was saying made any sense at all to me. His words perfectly spoken, he continued.

"He will intercede. There will be no interference from any forces. You will take full control, and your life will come to a full circle. There, at that place, you will be satisfied and ready. With a blink of any eye, your responsibilities complete. And with honor we will all rejoice. For that time will come to pass. And I, Michael, will be waiting. That is what I said to Natasto, Rachel, back at Maximillion's."

I looked at Michael not saying a word because none of what he had just said made any sense to me at all. Standing in front of me with his arms still folded in front of him, he said, "Rachel, I just repeated to you the law that was given to me. The laws of your life. What I said to Natasto."

"Why?" I asked.

Michael unfolded his arms, placing his arms at his side while standing straight as if he were in a line on a battlefield with soldiers ready to take down the enemy threatening his existence. This was weird I thought.

"Michael, what was it that Natasto shouted back at you and Retsis before he left Maximillion's?"

"Rachel, Natasto shouted, 'I am Abaddon, Appolyon, the king of darkness the master of deception, and yes, I will kill, destroy all that is possible within my reach and within your reach.' I am sure, Rachel, that none of this makes any sense to you right now. When the time is right, it has been written even then you won't understand at the beginning. Until then, Rachel, you must travel with this holy stone from Jerusalem."

Michael reached down into his pocket pulling out the most beautiful silver and gold rock. The rock illuminated the entire room. I was afraid to touch the rock at first, and then Michael opened my hand and put his hand on top of my hand, allowing the rock to rest in the middle of my hand. I wrapped my fingers around the rock. As I held the stone tightly in my hand my heart began to increase in beats. The energy that I felt was overpowering so much that I dropped the stone on the floor.

"What are you doing, Rachel? You must not feel afraid," Michael said.

I closed my eyes tight as Michael placed the small stone in my hand once again. I took three deep breaths and began to feel that same feeling of peace that I felt the night that GiGi died. I no longer felt that strong surge of energy or fear. My body felt light in weight, and it was difficult for me to hold my head up straight. I felt beautiful and the definition of Utopia was now identified. I opened my eyes to see Michael lifting me out of the chair. He carried me over to my bed and put me in the bed gently. I felt as if I was weightless. I did not even feel my body touch the mattress; I felt like I was floating in mid air. I could hear Michael speaking to someone else in the room in another language as I fell into a deep sleep. Whatever was happening to me, I truly had no control over.

CHAPTER
SEVEN

The next morning I woke up late. I looked at the clock at my bedside it was 10 a.m., and I felt groggy. I looked around my room, and I realized that I was supposed to have been in chemistry class two hours ago. I jumped out of bed, ran to the bathroom, and jumped into the shower. My chemistry class was to let out in 10 minutes. I knew that I would never make it to that class in just 10 minutes, but I needed to see Natasto today. I could not bear to have to wait until Monday before seeing him again.

I had so many questions to ask him. Michael was here last night, and I could not remember the extent of our conversation or when he left the dorm room. I hurried out of the shower after washing my hair. Throwing a towel around my body, I rushed to my clothes closet, grabbing a pair of blue jeans and a T-shirt, and began dressing.

Just as I pulled the T-shirt over my head, I realized, when I looked at the clock, that my chemistry class was just letting out. I sat on the edge of the bed feeling frustrated. I looked over at the desk and noticed a small gold and silver stone. I ran out of my room down the stairs to try and catch Natasto coming out of our chemistry class.

Finally it hit me. Yesterday! Natasto had some explaining to do. I ran as fast as I could to Nelson Hall, where our chemistry class was held. I was beginning to remember bits and pieces of yesterday.

The classroom was empty. Totally frustrated, I returned to my room to pick up my books for the remaining classes of the day. This meant that I had to wait until Monday before I would see Natasto in class again, unless Natasto made an effort to find me.

During the entire two hours and ten minutes that I sat in my biology class, it was difficult for me to focus on what the instructor was saying. And at that moment right before the bell rang, Professor Roderick said, "Rachel, what do you think the right answer would be?"

"I'm sorry Professor Roderick. Can you repeat the question?"

"Yes, How would you explain the process of the cellular exchanges between the electrolytes potassium and sodium in our bodies, and how it affects our organs?"

I looked at Professor Roderick and the answer came right to me, "Potassium is the major cation in intracellular fluid. Its functions include maintenance of the regular cardiac rhythm, transmission and conduction of our nerve impulses, and use of glucose by our cells. Sodium is the major cation of our extra cellular fluid. It assists with the production and transmission of nerve impulses also. The sodium regulates our osmotic pressure and controls the distribution of water throughout our bodies. Sodium also helps to balance our blood pressure."

I looked at Professor Roderick, hoping that the answer was correct.

"Correct. That was a great way to explain the process at the cellular exchange level."

I smiled at Professor Roderick and said, "Thank you."

The strange thing about this exchange was that I never knew the answer to that question. It just popped into my head. Life was not making sense to me anymore. I felt as if I was either losing control or losing my mind. The two people in the world that I trusted the most seemed to have changed personalities on me. Class was over; I felt exhausted physically and mentally and decided to go back to the room for a quick nap. I had time because my next class didn't start for another two hours.

On my walk back to the dorm, I bumped into Retsis. She was walking with her theology instructors who she introduced to me as Professor Daniel and Professor Gabriel. Professor Daniel looked familiar to me.

I asked, "Professor Daniel, have we met in the past?"

He responded, "I'm not sure. Have we?"

I shrugged my shoulders and answered, "I don't know, but you look awfully familiar to me."

Retsis interrupted, "Rachel, Professor Gabriel is my Italian instructor."

I smiled extended my hand to shake his hand. Professor Gabriel said, "I am trying to encourage Retsis and Michael, my best students, to speak to each other in Italian to enhance their pronunciations of the dialect."

I looked at Retsis and smiled. She smiled back at me. What a relief, I thought. Michael and Retsis were telling the truth. Now things started making sense again.

Professor Daniel said, "What a great combination theology and Italian."

Retsis quickly interjected, "This is all exciting, Rachel. Michael and I get to take a trip next semester to the Vatican in Italy, where we will meet with the Pope. We will have the opportunity to address many questions regarding Christianity and its history in the Catholic religion."

Retsis began asking Professor Daniel about certain details of the trip to Rome. While answering Rachel's questions, Professor Daniel stopped walking and stood in front of us, while continuing to answer Retsis' questions. It suddenly dawned on me that Professor Daniel resembled the man who attended GiGi's funeral several years ago-that unknown man who wore that black suit, had the pasty-colored skin, and sat in the back of the church during GiGi's funeral services. I didn't mention to Professor Daniel anything about his resemblance to this man. I continued to listen tentatively as he spoke.

"That sounds interesting," I said.

Retsis said, "You're right, it is interesting."

Before the two professors walked off, Professor Daniel said, in a deep voice, "It isn't too late, Rachel, for you to change your major."

Professor Gabriel shook my hand once again and said, "This is nothing except history and the identification of the world prior to our generations, as well as its existence."

Professor Daniel and Professor Gabriel walked off in different directions. They were both tall and distinguished looking men.

"Retsis, how much money is that trip to Rome going to cost you and Michael?" I said.

"Not much, according to Professor Daniel. He says that most of the cost has been included in the scholarship."

"Wow! That's great."

"We have room for one more on the trip, Rachel, if you decide to take Professor Daniel up on his suggestion. You will just need to change your major from biochemistry to theology."

"I just may consider that offer, Retsis. I am intrigued with how the history of Italy ties into Christianity. What type of job could I get after I graduate with a degree in theology?"

"Rachel, you can teach theology or Italian, minister to a congregation or maybe teach ethics. There are many professions attached to theology."

The next six weeks at Yale came and went. The semester was over. I never saw Natasto in chemistry class again. When I inquired about Natasto to the chemistry instructor, he said that Natasto had dropped the course. This just confirmed the fact that he truly had no interest in pursuing a relationship with me.

What were Natastos intentions? Was he truly an evil man as Michael stated? Where did he come from, and where did he go? I had often thought about him as I sat in chemistry class, wondering if I would ever see him again. If I didn't see him again, it wouldn't matter anyway. My mind was somewhat made up to change my major of study. I had more important things on my mind now besides Natasto.

CHAPTER
EIGHT

Three weeks passed. After addressing many questions to Retsis and Michael about theology and job related opportunities, I was now convinced-without a doubt-that this was something that I also wanted to do. This was not just to reap the benefits of the trip but to extend what had already been a part of my life. If I didn't want to teach theology, I could teach ethics. Retsis and Michael had learned so much about the Bible in just two years here at Yale. It was quite impressive. Their knowledge was unlimited, and it enhanced all other areas of general knowledge and fine-tuned their outlook on life in general. They now were able to communicate with others, such as their friendly relationship with Professor Daniel and Professor Gabriel. This was quite different for them than the one-on-one relationship they shared. In the past, they seemed to have had limitations to the social side of their human nature. They were content in their small world that only included me.

I spoke with my guidance counselor, regarding the transfer of credits and curriculum. There didn't seem to be a problem at all. I also spoke with Professor Daniel, who was the dean of theological studies. All of my courses that I had taken in the last two years were transferable. By initiating this change of my major from Biochemistry to theology it would cost me about nine credits. I could live with that. Besides I had enough time to make these changes because the trip to Rome was scheduled for the first week in October until the last week in December, which was a couple of months away. The information that I received was that there was one vacant seat. This meant that there was enough room for me. I was elated.

I had decided, yes, I would go to Rome. I immediately made an appointment to meet with Professor Gabriel, who was the assistant to Professor Daniel. The earliest appointment to meet was two days hence. I needed to get started to begin this process of transfer from one course of study to another and to begin preparations for the trip. I couldn't wait to tell Retsis and Michael the great news. I knew that they were going to be just thrilled. I most certainly couldn't wait until tomorrow to inform them. I thought why wait until tomorrow? I decided to walk over to Maximillion's where they were scheduled to work tonight. Actually I began skipping to the café, I was so happy. My only concern about traveling with the group to Italy was that I didn't speak the language that was necessary to communicate and to successfully complete the course of study while in Rome. Realistically, it was a little too late for me to worry about learning Italian.

As I approached Maximillions, I could see Retsis behind the counter talking with Professor Daniel.

"Hello, Retsis," I said. " Hello, Professor Daniel."

"Hello, Rachel," Professor Daniel said at the same time as Retsis. I looked around the store, and I didn't see Michael.

"Where is Michael?" I asked.

Retsis answered, "Michael had to run an errand for Professor Daniel. He will be right back."

"Oh! OK" I sat down on the stool next to Professor Daniel.

Retsis said, "Rachel, I haven't seen you all day what's new?"

"Well, I'd rather wait until Michael returns before telling you what's new."

When Retsis wasn't looking, I whispered into Professor Daniel's ear, "Professor Daniel, did Professor Gabriel mention to you that I have decided to change my curriculum of major from biochemistry to theology?"

Professor Daniel looked at me and nodded his head no.

"Oh, that's good because I want the news to be a surprise to Retsis and Michael."

At that moment, Michael walked into Maximillion's.

"Rachel, how are you?" Michael asked while giving me the tightest hug.

"I can't breathe, Michael," I said.

Michael joking smiled and loosened his grip from around my waist.

"Now that you have returned Michael, I have some great news for you and Retsis. In two days, I will officially be apart of your theology group."

"Oh that is fantastic," Michael and Retsis said simultaneously. Retsis came from behind the counter, where she had been standing, and gave me the warmest embrace. I began crying.

"How could you guys think for one minute that I would allow you two to travel to the other end of the world without me? After all we had been through together as best friends, inseparable for this long, why change things now?"

Professor Daniel said, "Rachel, I think they somehow knew that you would be taking this journey with them."

The three of us, Michael, Retsis and myself huddled in a circle for about five minutes.

"What a wise decision," Professor Daniel said.

Retsis looked at her watch and said, "Ten minutes to closing. Why don't we go and get a bite to eat someplace nice you guys?"

"That sounds great! And I am treating you all since I am the one with all of the money, and I don't have to work," I said.

Michael began mimicking my voice, "I am treating since I am the one with all of the money, and I don't have to work. I wish we all were so lucky, Rachel."

We found a really nice place to eat called Barimores near the campus on Lyons Street. We exchanged classroom stories after dinner. The food was terrific and so was the evening. It turned out to be a beautiful night for walking and talking.

We must have walked for about thirty minutes after dinner. The night was beautiful; the sky was clear. There must have been over a million stars in the sky. And the night dew had began to set in the grass as our feet got wet walking thorough the grassy areas around campus. I thought that this would be the perfect opportunity to request a few private lessons from Retsis and Michael in Italian. Such as hello, goodbye, how are you, yes and no. The basics just enough to get me by.

"Retsis, you and Michael are going to have to help me learn to speak Italian. Otherwise I will not be able to communicate and function on the trip at the same level as the both of you."

Retsis responded, "Yes, you will, Rachel. For now just purchase some cassette tapes. Those will teach you the basics. All you need is just enough to get by," she said.

CHAPTER
NINE

A week before the trip, everything was set. I was ready to see Italy now that my passport and visa had arrived. Yet, I had some loose ends to tie up. I desperately had the urge to visit GiGi's grave before taking this journey. This visit was going to be a first for me. After GiGi died Pastor Neil thought it would be best for me not to go to the grave site. Respecting his wishes as power of attorney, I didn't attend the burial service. Arrangements were made for me to stay with the sisters of the church after the funeral service was over. Besides, I wanted to remember GiGi the way that she was, when she was alive.

If I was going to visit her grave, I knew I had better visit as soon possible due to the limited time that I had before traveling abroad. With New York not too far away, I could shop and visit the grave site in one day. Although, I knew that she wasn't there, all that was in that grave was the shell of her body. Her soul, I believed, was at rest. This concept helped me to accept what I couldn't change: her death. Calling the Metro North Station to get the schedule of trains going into New York and returning to New Haven, allowed me to better plan my day. The first train out was 8:15 a.m., which was great for me.

Leaving early would give me enough time to first shop uptown before continuing on up to the Bronx, where the cemetery was located. I turned in early for the night so that I would be well rested for the journey to New York. Before turning in, I telephoned Retsis and Michael to inform them of my trip to the city. I didn't want any company on this journey. They understood and wished me a safe trip.

I set my alarm clock for six o' clock in the morning. I made a list of last-minute items to pick up for the trip while in New York. After making out a short list of items to pick up, including Italian/American cassette tapes, I turned on my small black and white television to watch the news. I turned to channel five, which was a New York channel.

My intentions were to check out the weather forecast for the morning. My timing in turning on the television could not have been better. A gunman in New York had just murdered sixty-six people with a semi-automatic machine gun. He had not been captured and the New York City SWAT team had no clue of what sent this thirty-two year old man to the rooftop of a condominium located in the middle of Times Square. With a negotiator on his way to the rooftop where the gunman was at large, all one could hope for was the safety of the negotiator and a safe take down of the gunman at large. The news commentator was calling this situation the worst massacre since the Bombing of the Courthouse on Lafayette Street last year on December 3, 1967.

Whether they caught this guy or not, my mind was already made up to go to New York. The news continued as I dozed off to sleep. I quickly awakened to a jolt of electricity that seemed to have hit my body, sending my body about two inches off of my bed. I didn't feel any pain. I jumped out of bed, looked out of the window to see if it was raining outside, thinking, perhaps I was struck by a small bolt of lightning. No rain. No lightning. I didn't know what had happened to me. Maybe it was a dream. I turned the television off and fell to sleep.

Waking up to the sound of my alarm clock, I crawled out of bed and took a hot shower. While in the shower, I remembered dreaming about nurses and doctors surrounding my bed. Unable to remember any of the conversation amongst them, what I did remember was hearing the voice of GiGi saying, "Please, Lord. Don't let her die. You have already taken her sister, her mother. Please let her live." What a weird dream. What sister was she talking about? I had no sister. Was this GiGi's way of warning me not to take the trip to New York? I jumped out of the shower, quickly turned on the news for an update. I discovered, with much relief, that the sniper was in police custody. That news was reassuring. I quickly got dressed and caught a taxi cab to the Metro north train station.

Bright and early, I arrived at the New Haven Station and caught the 8:15 train just as planned. The ride to New York didn't take long. Before I knew it, the conductor called out, "Penn Station, last stop." This was exciting being in New York again. It had been about two years since I was here last. I walked up the stairs out of the station and decided to walk over to Thirty-fourth Street to shop instead of traveling uptown.

After going in and out of the many shops, I picked up all the items on my list. Two nice shirts and two ties for Michael. A pair of shoes and a dress for Retsis. I passed by a little florist shop and picked up some roses for GiGi's grave. Sure, I knew that she couldn't smell them; however, putting the flowers on her grave made me feel better. The entire shopping spree took me two and a half hours to complete. I hailed a cab up to the Bronx to Fairfield Cemetery. I handed the cab driver a fifty dollar bill and asked him if he would return in a half hour to pick me up to take me back downtown. He was happy about the large tip and agreed to pick me up to take me back downtown. There was no way that I was going to miss that last train back to New Haven.

The cemetery was huge, and I did not notice anyone else visiting. I walked over to GiGi's grave and I stood looking at her headstone that read,

"Gwenith Gallo Born July 20 1895 died October 16, 1963." I felt so sad and empty. I wish that I had gotten the opportunity to attend the burial service after GiGi had died. This trip might have been easier for me to handle. The headstone next to GiGi's read,

"Margaret-Monty-Legna Born December 7, 1929 Died April 20, 1947 / Beloved Sister Legna, born April 20, 1947 Died April 20, 1947." Wow! I didn't know when GiGi was buried after the funeral that my mom's body lied right next to hers. Oh my, God. It hit me that Sister Legna born on my birthday and died on my birthday. I had a twin Sister who died at birth. That couldn't be. Grandmother never mentioned to me that I had a twin sister. Why would she keep that a secret? What else did she conveniently fail to tell me? I knew that my dad died in the Korean War, and I had no clue where he was buried. This explained why I always felt as if a part of me was missing. The feeling of emptiness that had invaded my inner space made no sense up until now. It was my other half that was

missing, my twin sister. I knelt down on my knees between both graves and began to pray out loud.

"I miss you, GiGi. You never told me that I had a twin sister who died at birth. I guess you felt that the time just wasn't right for me to know. And Momma, oh Momma. You were so young to have been snatched away by death at such an early age of eighteen. You and GiGi, Momma, are both with sister, and I am left behind here to mend fences in this crazy world alone. Well, I'll tell you, momma, God must have something planned for me. For the good Lord to leave me here without you and GiGi, he must have some serious work planned for me here. GiGi, you never did meet Retsis. You slipped right out on me that evening that she came over to the house to meet you. And my best friend, Michael, GiGi, you sent him here to me for my protection. I still feel so empty inside. You must help me find my way here in this old crazy world. GiGi, you made a start by leaving me all of that money. I invested most of it into mutual funds. GiGi, how could you have afforded such an extravagant insurance policy? We lived so tight financially on your fixed income. Well anyway, I'm going on a trip to Italy. This is why I needed to visit you guys before leaving. I will be gone for three months."

I looked up at the sky, and at that moment I saw three fluffy white clouds—two big clouds and one small cloud. In the middle of each cloud, I saw a smiling face. That was my confirmation that my family was with me.

The sky looked like it was quickly turning gray. The smiling faces no longer peeped through the clouds. I quickly picked up my purse that I had placed down on GiGi's grave. As I stood to my feet, I could see a man quickly running from behind a large oak tree that was on the far right side of momma and sister's grave.

This man, dressed in black was tall and slender. If I didn't know any better, I would have sworn that it was Natasto. The man had the same body frame, and the side view of his face remarkably resembled Natasto's face. I knew that this could not be, simply because Natasto new nothing about my family.

I quickly walked out of the cemetery and caught the first taxi cab over to Penn Station to catch the Metro North train to New Haven, Connecticut. I couldn't wait for my cab driver to return. That would have meant waiting another 15 minutes. I'm sure that he would understand why I couldn't wait in the rain. Besides, he was paid in advance.

I couldn't wait to tell Michael and Retsis about my new revelation. The train ride back to New Haven, Connecticut, was exceptionally long. I dozed off to sleep a couple of times, and finally I heard the conductor say, "New Haven, this stop is New Haven." I jumped up and quickly stepped off of the train.

Retsis and Michael were waiting for me outside of the train terminal. I ran toward where they were standing.

"Retsis, how did you and Michael know that I was on that train?"

Retsis answered, " We took a chance and came over here hoping that you would be on that train."

CHAPTER
TEN

While waiting for a taxicab, I couldn't wait to inform Retsis and Michael about my journey to New York. I handed them the bags with their gifts inside and made them promise me that they wouldn't look inside the bag until we returned to campus. They both agreed. I began telling the two of them about my trip.

"Guess what I found out today?" The both of them looked at me with a look of we already know what you are going to say. I began telling them all about my experience at the cemetery.

"I had a twin sister that died at birth, and get a load of this, her name was Sister Legna."

"Was she a nun?" Michael asked.

I said, "No, she died at birth. Her first name was Sister and her last name of course was the same as mine Legna."

"You have got to be kidding," Michael said.

"No, Michael, I am not kidding."

Retsis asked, "Your grandmother never mentioned that you had a twin sister?"

"No, Retsis, and I don't know why."

Retsis had nothing else to say. She was quiet and preoccupied with her thoughts during the entire ride back to the dorm. I needed to distract Retsis from her deep thoughts so I asked, "Retsis, are you getting nervous about flying next week?"

"I've flown dozens of times in the past."

"Oh really, I didn't know that."

I asked, "What about you, Michael? Are you getting cold feet about flying?"

"Like Retsis, I've also flown many times in the past," he said.

"I guess I'm the only one who will need a sedative before take off."

Retsis and Michael looked at each other and began laughing.

Michael said, "Truly, Rachel, flying isn't that bad. Just think of yourself with wings, flying high and having full control of the galaxy and the universe. All you have to do is let go and go with it, and the gravity of the atmosphere will balance your weight."

I smiled and said, "Michael, you have such a way with words. By the way, where will we live for the three months while we're in Rome? I didn't get the chance to look at the itinerary in full."

Retsis said, "We will be staying at a hotel."

"I thought that we were going to stay with a family."

Retsis responded, "No, Professor Daniel and Professor Gabriel thought that it would be best for us to stay at a hotel. This would allow the group to remain together and to have more flexibility of time. The name of the hotel where we are scheduled to stay for the three months is The Hotel Rinasciment. This hotel stands in the heart of Rome near the Vatican. The address is Via Del Pellegrino, 122-00186 Roma."

I asked Retsis and Michael, "How will you two be able to afford to live in this hotel for three months?" I knew Maximillion's where they worked only paid minimum wage; therefore, their savings could not have been adequate to compensate for their basic needs for the next three months.

Retsis answered, "Professor Daniel has picked up our expenses."

"Please Retsis I don't want Professor Daniel picking up my portion of the tab. I thought that this trip was picked up financially by our scholarship money," I said.

"Yes it is." Michael quickly answered. "There are just a couple of expenses that the scholarship is not going to cover. Minor expenses that is."

"Please, I would be happy to help you guys out financially while we're in Rome," I said.

The next seven days flew by as we continued to prepare for take-off. I couldn't accomplish enough in one day. I began cramming last-minute details of studying and completing papers. I wanted to have the two days before the trip all to myself to relax and do exactly what I wanted to do.

The next six days came and left with all accomplished that I had anticipated. And before we knew it, we were facing the night before departure.

CHAPTER
ELEVEN

It was the night before the trip to Italy, and Retsis and Michael decided to camp out in my room. We were all packed, excited and could not sleep. There was a group of 12 of us traveling from the United States. I knew two other girls in our group that I had met in the past. Retsis had introduced us. This was great because I knew two other students besides Retsis and Michael. God forbid if I should get lost in Rome, knowing two other people besides the professors, Michael, and Retsis would decrease my chances of remaining lost.

Michael decided to place all of our baggage on one side of the room for easy access in the morning. Everything was set for takeoff in the morning. We decided to camp out on the floor of my dormitory room. There was more than enough floor space. My room was about 20 feet wide and 25 feet long. Retsis and Michael had brought over their own blankets. That was great because I only had enough bedding for myself. This was the perfect time for me to ask any last minute questions regarding the purpose of our trip to Rome about the exact mission for three months and the expectations that were required of us.

Visiting the Vatican and having the opportunity to speak with the clergy, cardinals, and the pope as well as grasping the entire theological concept of the Catholic Church and its denomination was a tad bit broad of an understanding of what I was required to accomplish on a personal level. Now that I had Retsis and Michael in my territory, my dormitory room in a comfortable position, the time was right to narrow down my mission for the next three months. What was my exact mission for this journey to travel across the world?

The three of us had assumed our sleeping space on the floor. The fact that Michael was a guy never invaded our comfort zone. Michael was truly like a brother to Retsis and me.

"Michael, Retsis, besides addressing the routine and duties of the Catholic Church, studying religion from a broad spectrum, what is the ultimate objective of this trip?"

There was a moment of silence in the room. Michael responded after clearing his throat several times and began laughing. "Well Rachel, it took you long enough to ask. Retsis and I were beginning to think that you were just traveling along with us for the ride."

I sat up straight, looked over at Michael, and then turned my head to look over at Retsis. Retsis and Michael sat up straight. Retsis began speaking to Michael in Italian. "Oh no, not again. I really don't like when the two of you speak Italian, knowing that I haven't a clue to what you are saying. You guys, it's down right rude."

They stopped speaking in Italian, and Retsis said, "Michael, the time is right to tell her."

"Tell me what?" I said.

Michael took a deep breath, shook his head and began rubbing the front of his forehead with his hand. "All right, all right. I'll tell her."

"Rachel, we are going to Italy on instructions from Our Father."

I began laughing out loud. "No kidding. If your parents want you to get your degrees in theology after all the money they have spent on your education thus far," I said.

"No, Rachel. Listen. This is no joke. We were sent to assist you in locating the right path back. The right path back is to first have full knowledge of your creation. Visiting Rome and the Vatican would give you a crash course on Catholicism and its history. You will have the experience of cohabiting with nuns and priests from all walks of life at some point in your life. We don't know when, we are still waiting to find out."

Quickly responding, I said, "Yeah right, Michael, and we, or rather should I say, the twelve of us along with Professor Daniel and Professor Gabriel, are taking this trip for three months so that I can get a crash course on the Catholic denomination?"

I could see Retsis was serious by the expression on her face as she began to explain, "Rachel, I wanted to prepare you for this months ago; however, the time wasn't right. Everything on earth is accomplished according to timing."

I said, "How could you have wanted to tell me this months ago? You didn't know months ago that I would change my major from chemistry to theology."

Retsis said, "Yes we did, Rachel. We knew before you did because of your mission."

This was all crazy what Retsis and Michael were saying. I took a deep breath, looked at the both of them, and I knew by the expressions on their faces that they were serious. I suddenly became afraid of Retsis and Michael.

"You guys, I think this is over my head. I am not the one to assist you with this mission," I said.

"Yes you are," Michael said.

"And, we are assisting you. You are not assisting us," Retsis said.

I began to really feel frightened, I didn't understand what was happening, and I didn't understand why Retsis and Michael were beginning to take on the appearance of supernatural beings. As they both continued to speak to me, I could almost see through Michael's body at this point. Retsis was beautiful, and her glow was definitely not from this world. A bright golden orange glow filled the room. Her body radiated with such illuminus light of gold that it was difficult for me to look at her.

Michael jumped to his feet and walked over to my desk, where I had placed the stone the night that he had come over to enlightened me about Natasto's character. He picked up the small stone opened my hand and placed it in my palm. Retsis watched. I closed my hand, squeezing the small stone with all of the strength that I had. I don't know what made me squeeze the stone. I felt strong; I felt as if I had been reborn, reborn, with supernatural powers.

I stood, held my head back, took a deep breath, and suddenly all fear was gone. I continued to squeeze the stone and suddenly everything made sense. I looked over at Michael and asked, "Are you my guardian angel Michael? He smiled and nodded his head.

"I am one of your guardian angels," he said.

I took another deep breath, looked over at Retsis, and asked, "Are you Sister?"

Retsis stood to her feet and looked at me smiled. She said, "Yes, I am Retsis Legna. I am your sister. I am your Sister Angel in the flesh. Retsis Legna is Sister Angel if you reverse the spelling. I have always been here for you. In your deepest times of troubles and distress, I have never left you, Rachel. I was at your side when you were born and entered into this world. Michael has helped me with my exit after you were born on April 20, 1947. However, September 30 1955, was the first day that you and I met in the flesh. Remember that little girl that called out your name in the midst of you losing control of your bouncing red ball in the street? On the corner of 23rd street and Lexington Avenue?"

I was unable to answer. This occurred many years ago. How did she know this? My mind was racing. Was she there?

With the small stone in my hand, I continued to feel that sense of serenity, peace, and utopia the way I imagined Utopia to be. With my eyes closed and head tilted back, I continued to listen to Retsis. I was repeating over and over in my mind: My God, My God, My Lord, My redeemer, My strength."

Retsis called out my name in the same tone and whispering sounding voice as she did that first day that we met 14 years ago.

"Rachel," repeating the call to me again, "Rachel."

I quickly thought back in retrospect to that day when I first met Retsis. Retsis most certainly saved my life. If she had not called out my name to distract me from stepping off of the sidewalk and walking into the street, I would have been hit by that speeding car that was coming around the corner at about ninety miles per hour.

"Your grandmother's death, Rachel. Yes, I was there," Retsis said, while Michael looked on with his arms folded in front of his chest. "I was even there at Monty's passing. Through my travels as I got older, according to your space and time, I met Monty. My Father, who I told you about many times, is also your father. He is our Father in heaven."

It was beginning to make a little more sense. "Retsis, I guess that's how your father knew my mother because he is our Father."

Retsis responded, "Yes, Rachel, that is right."

I said, "Retsis, you were never introduced to GiGi before she died."

Retsis said, "And that was purposely orchestrated. If you had ever introduced me to your grandmother, Rachel, she would have immediately known that I was a supernatural being. Your grandmother would have known immediately that I was your guardian angel. Your grandmother's relationship with spirituality and our Father was the closest thing to her being in heaven. I met Gwenith Gallo, or as you called her GiGi, many times. It is all about timing here. Rachel, your time on earth is different from our time spiritually. September 30th 1955, was when I first met you Rachel. Your life imminently usable, without a doubt by the laws of man. Rachel, it has been written in the book of life that you were supposed to be here. Our Father decided to use you because he knows what we know not. This is your mission from him. Your body is his vessel, and right now it is pure. At 21 years of age you are still a virgin. You don't drink and you don't smoke. Rachel, you have not adapted to the many sins of the world. He has chosen you with our help to intercede with the process of preserving the world and its land and people."

Michael interjected, "After your grandmother died Rachel, you heard a voice."

I looked at Michael, thinking Wow! That is right. "Yes," I said. "I heard a voice and it said for me to fret not that I have been sent a mighty warrior."

Michael began quoting the rest of what was said to me on the evening GiGi died:

"Fret not, my child. I will grant you such fruitful rewards. Let not your troubles blind you, for I have sent a mighty warrior for you to follow and gain strength from."

I interrupted him and asked, "Michael are you the mighty warrior?"

Michael continued to repeat verbatim what was said, in the same tone of voice that I had heard that night, "You must begin to prepare yourself for the unthinkable. Never wither in faith for I have chosen you."

"And all of this time I thought that was a dream. Perhaps I am the chosen one. Why me? Is it because of the many prayers that were sent up to the heavens by GiGi?"

Neither, Retsis or Michael answered my question.

Retsis said, "Rachel, you must not lose focus of your mission. We are here to assist you. You were chosen to save many lives."

CHAPTER
TWELVE

At that moment, there was a knock at the door, a loud knock at my door. Michael walked over to the door, opened it as if he knew in advance who was on the other side. There stood Professor Daniel. I looked over at my clock on the desk, and it was 10:47 p.m. Professor Daniel entered my room, behind him was Professor Gabriel.

"The trip to Italy has been canceled. We don't have much time; her body is beginning to fail," Professor Daniel said in a shaky voice.

Professor Gabriel looked at Michael and Retsis and said, "You know what this means right?"

Retsis said, "Yes, this means that instead of traveling to Italy for the crash course and a look into the future, we will remain here to complete this task."

Professor Gabriel said, "Does she know?"

I didn't hesitate to answer, "Yes I know. I know that I was put on earth to assist you all with the take down of evil while preserving the lives of others. That is with the help of two archangels, Daniel and Gabriel, and my personal guardian angel, Michael, and let me not forget my twin sister, Retsis, who has left me alone for the past 21 years of my life."

Retsis looked at me and said, "Rachel, you were never alone. I was with you from the beginning of time, that is your time, and I will remain by your side until the end."

I smiled and said, "That's right, you were with me, all through out junior high school and high school. I just didn't know that you were my sister. All of this time, I thought that I had no family."

Retsis stretched out her arm and pointed her finger at me. She said, "Now wait a minute, Rachel. This is unfair. I was with you even before junior high school. We entered this world at the same time."

Professor Gabriel interrupted, "This is not the time for sibling rivalry."

"No, you are right. It is not. Professor Gabriel, let's be frank. Before you entered into this room you knew that Michael and Retsis had informed me of everything. I guess it just made you feel more comfortable on a mortal level to confirm, right?" I said.

Gabriel didn't answer my question. Instead he chose to lecture all of us on remaining focused on why we were here. "You all are forgetting why we are here. Professor Daniel just mentioned to you about our friend in the convalescent home. Her physical body is beginning to fail. In order to accomplish an adequate spiritual vessel to save the many lives that are at risk of being cut short due to evil, we must move quick. We need to get Rachel to the place where she could get back with all of the memories required to intercede destruction."

I was totally lost to what I was supposed to do here. I put the beautiful stone that I had been squeezing in my hand, which had gotten use to the prints of my fingers and palms, on the desk. The small stone had mercy on me this second time around by not sapping all of my energy, leaving me standing and awake. This time I was grateful.

Michael said, "Rachel, now that you know your purpose and some of what we are up against, you must not ever walk without the stone. You must carry it wherever you go. It is the only thing that could give you the strength to protect yourself against the evil forces that are most sure to attempt to destroy you."

I placed the stone inside of my purse.

Retsis said, "They have attempted to destroy you many times in the past, and they are waiting for the opportunity to succeed. They know who you are my darling sister."

"Remember how clever Natasto's was Rachel?" Michael said.

I looked at Michael; all of a sudden it hit me.

"Yes, that handsome man who so mysteriously appeared in my chemistry class," I said.

Retsis said, " have you figured out who he was? Thanks to Michael and I you still have your heart and your virginity. We literally prevented you from sleeping with the devil." Retsis, looking me straight in the eyes without any facial expression of emotions, continued to speak, "You see how clever he was, Rachel. He appeared in the form of a man that he knew you would be attracted to. Rachel, you are a female and you are in the flesh."

"If Natasto had succeeded in winning your heart, all of our chances of saving the many lives that are due to perish could not have been saved. They would have been lost," Michael said.

Retsis, raising both eyebrows, asked me, "Do you know who

Natasto is Rachel?"

I didn't hesitate to answer, while Professor Daniel, Professor Gabriel, and Michael tentatively looked and listened on. The room was filled with silence. I felt like I was being chastised for being human. "Yes, Natasto is To Satan reversed."

I was beginning to feel lightheaded. The stress of the day had finally caught up to me. My physical body feeling weary from the release of the stone that had pumped me up with an instant surge of energy, the energy required to understand the true purpose of my being. I was physically drained.

I sat down on my bed. As soon as I sat down, Professor Daniel insisted that we all gather our belongings and head quickly to New York to see Cardinal Cardonni Jessepe.

I asked, "Who is Cardinal Jessepe?"

Daniel said, "He is the cardinal of the Catholic Church in New York City."

"I hate to inform you guys, but I cannot do this. I'm not Catholic."

"Rachel, I hate to burst your bubble, but neither are we. We fall under no denomination. Besides, Rachel, we were there when you were baptized. You see my chosen one, why you were chosen. Why it has to be you?"

"Thanks a lot, Daniel, for letting me know that."

"You are quite welcome my dear."

Daniel yelled out, "We must gather our belongings right now, just a few things and call a driver to take us to New York. We don't have much time before the clock of life ticks its last beat. Cardinal Jessepe is waiting. He has tried to take her life twice in one week. Once he realizes that we are on to him, this could be extremely dangerous for Rachel."

"Who is he that you are referring to Professor Daniel? And whose life did he try to take twice in one week?" I asked.

Daniel said let me answer Rachel's questions.

"Rachel, we are not privy to disclose all of the details of what appears to you to be a weird, and strange predicament. Everything that you need to know you will find out as the days go by on a need-to-know basis. You are not ready yet, and our intentions here are not to frighten you to death. This is way above your head. Your spiritual comprehension is not at the level to precisely decipher what is most important and what is not. Take one day at a time and eventually it will all come together. Cardinal Cardonni Jessepe has been following the travels of your path for many years now, and so have I."

Gabriel said, "He will instruct you Rachel on what you need to know and the amount of time you have to know it."

Daniel said, "We must hurry to New York to meet the cardinal, in New York who is also the Arch Bishop. Once we arrive, he will instruct us on how to proceed assisting Rachel with her transfer. It must be carefully planned out. It is said that we have one and only one attempt to complete this Mission. How we will complete it is totally up to you, Rachel, and the Cardinal."

I grabbed my purse, a few clothes out of the suitcase that was already packed. Afterall I had no intentions of being gone long. I knew enough at this point that this was serious business and was willing to follow directions to remain safe. I was not ready to die. Retsis and Michael also grabbed a few pieces of clothing from their suitcases. Professor Gabriel was using the telephone to call a taxi. I wondered what cab driver would be willing to take this journey to New York at this hour of night? Also, what kind of cab driver didn't mind driving all the way from New Haven, Connecticut, to Manhattan at 11:54 p.m.? I answered that question myself: A crazy cab driver who was in desperate need of money.

Now awaiting a taxicab, the five of us stood in the middle of my dorm room and held hands forming a circle while Professor Daniel said a prayer. He quoted a scripture from the book of Daniel.

After prayer, we quickly left the room. I locked my door and proceeded down the stairs with Michael, Retsis, Professor Gabriel, and Professor Daniel. When we got outside the building I couldn't believe there was a yellow cab waiting in front of the building, It just didn't make sense that someone was willing to drive the five of us to Manhattan at midnight.

"We should arrive in New York in about one hour and forty five minutes," Professor Gabriel said, as we climbed into the taxi.

CHAPTER
THIRTEEN

During most of the car ride, Professor Daniel and Professor Gabriel spoke in Italian. Sure Retsis and Michael understood the conversation; however, I didn't understand. The cab driver never said two words. I sat in the back seat of the cab with Retsis, Michael and Professor Gabriel. Suddenly, I thought about the rest of the students who were scheduled to go to Rome with us. What were they going to do now that the trip was canceled?

I asked Professor Daniel and Professor Gabriel about the other students. Professor Daniel quickly interrupted me, "Rachel, please, you no longer have to refer to me as Professor Daniel or to Professor Gabriel as Professor Gabriel. Call me Daniel."

Professor Gabriel said, "Call me Gabriel."

I obliged by smiling and nodding my head. Daniel said that the entire trip was canceled for now. The nine students were notified by telephone. Gabriel had informed them of the sudden change of plans. Without giving them the full details regarding the urgency to cancel, they were informed with enough information to allow compliance and acceptance of our decision. Gabriel looked at me and said, "we may need their help later on also with this project. Without divulging all of the information regarding this mission, the student's expertise in theological studies could be utilized indirectly at some point of this mission to our benefit."

Gabriel did mention to the nine students that they were now officially on standby and to wait for further details and instructions from Professor Daniel. Daniel turned around, looked at me in the back seat and said, "Rachel, I hope you understand that it is you who will lead this operation. It is you who were chosen, before your time, to carry out this plan with us."

I didn't know what to say. Why me? I thought to myself once again. Why was I the one responsible for such a dangerous life-threatening task? I knew nothing about all of this. If I fail, will I have the blood of the world on my hands? My mind was racing. Besides, Daniel and Gabriel knew exactly how all of this would turn out in advance. Why couldn't they take care of this worldwide problem without me?

I have read the book of Daniel many times with GiGi. The book of Daniel was GiGi's favorite book in the Bible. Now I know why. I can remember reading along with GiGi the book of Daniel, night after night.

My mind quickly racing, back to GiGi's favorite scriptures. I could hear her soft spoken voice change octaves as she emphasized words that were most important to her.

Daniel turned back around and looked at me He said, " Everything will fall into place Rachel. All of those questions will be answered for you. Your edification will become clearer after our meeting with Cardinal Jessepe."

It was apparent Daniel and Gabriel could also read my mind. They knew everything that I was thinking, along with what I was feeling. While the cab driver continued to drive, I noticed that the speedometer was increasing. I looked at the cab driver as he looked at me through his rearview mirror. The car suddenly began to decrease in speed. Gabriel looked over at me, winked his eye and smiled.

I was beginning to feel better about this situation. A feeling of acceptance by no other alternative set in. Yes, it was I, Rachel; I was the chosen one. Sure I was frightened, but I knew that I had strange feelings my entire life that I was different. I couldn't understand what the difference was. Through out the years, I would compare my desires and priorities of life with my peers, and the similarities were few. The question that I had repeatedly asked myself over and over again through out the years was why was I so different?

I placed my head on Retsis' shoulder and closed my eyes again. I began to reminisce back to when I was a little girl, my daily ritual living with GiGi, and waking up in the morning and praying to get a good start on the day. GiGi insisted in starting out every morning with prayer.

Putting God first was always in our apartment. It was almost as if GiGi knew in advance that she was preparing me for this day. Not mentioning to me that I had a twin sister, reading every chapter to me from the book of Daniel night after night I knew that I had to find out what was missing from this picture. Introducing me to Daniel and Gabriel through the Bible long before this day was no coincidence.

Watching GiGi walk out of her little closet everyday confirmed her strong faith in what she believed. Her little secret place of the most high, where she secured her everlasting oath with God was refreshing and added faith to my beliefs when I too entered the room, which was seldom. Promising him her life has now become my big objective to seal her deal that she initiated long before my existence. I heard a voice, and I opened my eyes. It was Retsis. "Rachel, we're here. Wake up."

"I'm not sleeping," I said.

The cab pulled up in front of a huge brownstone church with a large steeple. It was absolutely beautiful. I looked out of the window of the cab and up at the sky. The rain began to pour out of the sky as if someone was emptying a container of water over the earth. Daniel paid the cab driver after we exited the vehicle and the driver sped off.

We walked up the steps, tried to open the double doors, and found they were locked. Professor Daniel told us to wait out front under the roof's ledge to prevent us from getting drenched. Just as Daniel went to the back of the church, the front door opened. There stood a nun, a old woman wearing a smile. This old woman had a beautiful smile; she looked as if she could have been at least 90 years old. Her smile put me at ease, and I suddenly felt welcomed to this new environment.

We entered the church as this woman motioned us to. Daniel walked up from the inside of the other end of the church with Cardinal Cardonni Jessepe. Daniel motioned us to follow him. Before we followed him, the old nun knelt down at my feet. She began speaking in Italian while making a sign of the cross with her hand across her chest. She stood to her feet and began talking to Retsis. I reached inside of my purse to get my stone. Not because I felt threatened or unsafe but because I wanted to get to the place spiritually where I was back in my room at the university.

Suddenly holding the stone in my hand, I began to join in on the conversation in Italian. It was perfectly clear to me what was being said.

Retsis looked at me and smiled. "It's about time you start to catch on, Rachel."

I knew at this point that I was truly the vessel chosen to bring down destruction that had been planned by evil forces. I was no longer reluctant; however, I was prepared mentally to receive my instructions to begin this mission.

As I looked around the inside of the church, I could see that the decor was not contemporary. The decor and structure was a representation of history. In old dark wood, the carvings intricately told a story of its mere existence. All of the colors were earth colors, browns oranges, and greens; however, they just appeared quite deeper through my eyes. Nothing was appearing normal anymore.

Michael motioned me to follow him, Gabriel, and Daniel to the room where Cardinal Jessepe had designated, for our meeting. Entering the large room in which was clearly a study surrounded by walls of books, my mind, body, and spirit were ready to receive information and instructions on the commencement of my duties. Cardinal Jessepe motioned me to sit. His reverence and demeanor was one of the highest spiritually that I had experienced. His holiness radiated just as Daniel and Gabriel's holiness radiated when they spoke. His presence gave off strong spiritual vibes that could be felt within my body.

Cardinal Cardonni Jessepe looked like a clever man who held much of his life's experiences on the outside of his face, identified by many lines around his eyes and mouth. He had to be at least seventy years old. His eyeglasses sat at the edge of his nose as he looked above them while speaking to us. His voice was deep with bass, and every word spoken was perfectly pronounced. He was a tall man, just as tall as Gabriel and Daniel at a little over six feet tall. He was slender in weight, just like Daniel and Gabriel. Cardinal

Cardonni Jessepe began speaking to me directly, as his eyes were on me alone. My heart was pounding.

"Hello, Rachel. I am Cardinal Cardonni Jessepe. I'm sure you know why Daniel, Gabriel, Retsis, and Michael were sent here, and why they escorted you here tonight. It has been written many years ago that after the start of the tribulation period, the midpoint that is, there would be sent to us a man. This man wearing the sign of the beast in the symbolic numbers of three sixes, almost impossible to detect. But, what we know for sure is that he is the son of perdition. Meaning that he is of eternal damnation, hell. Everything that is holy and of the word, he is totally against. We have identified him as the Beast, Satan, Lucifer." The cardinal wearing a long black robe with a turtle neck underneath added to his conservative personality. After speaking, I noticed his left eyebrow would rise up.

Looking directly at me the cardinal continued to speak, "The Devil will represent himself as the Prince of this world. I know that he will have authority over every religion, Jews, Gentiles, Protestants, Catholics, and the Islamic faith in order to achieve his worldwide dominion if we allow it. He will proclaim his own deity that causes loneliness, misery amongst all men. If we allow it." Pacing the floor of the study while twisting a pencil around in his right hand and making eye contact with me after every sentence, he continued. Michael, Retsis, Gabriel, and Daniel looked on quietly without interruption.

"I say unto you my daughter, Rachel, if you have any doubts, if you have any second thoughts, now is the time to voice them. Our father has given us a free will. You have been chosen because of your purity, your walk thus far throughout life has been filled with trials and tribulations. You have succeeded in overcoming them all for the first seven years of your life. Your grandmother has set a strong holy foundation beneath your feet. However, if there is any lack of faith or fear of failure you will fail at this mission, and that would be devastating to all of the lives that are presently in jeopardy. There are four hundred and forty four lives due to die at the hands of murderers that chose evil over good. You are going to intercede and preserve the four hundred and forty four lives.

You won't accomplish this with any weapons or any army. This will be carried out through word of mouth."

My spiritual warriors—Retsis, Daniel, Michael, and Gabriel— nodded their heads in agreement with what the cardinal was saying. I looked up at the cardinal and began to speak from my heart. The tears began to flow from my eyes; I dropped to my knees.

"Father, I have sinned. I am not perfect, considering that I am in the flesh. I have tried to walk your walk and to live the life of a good person. In missing church services on Sundays and not living up to what I have been taught by my grandmother, I have fallen short, Father. And with the feelings of lust at a point in my life of uncertainty, he came to me in the image of a man I couldn't resist on my own. I am so sorry. Forgive me, Father, for I have sinned." Continuing to cry and beg for forgiveness, I looked up at everyone through my tears and said, "I was taught that confession was good for the soul. This is my first confession out loud. One thing that I know is that I have always loved my Lord, from the depths of my soul to the bottom of my heart."

CHAPTER
FOURTEEN

I felt a jolt of electricity go through my body, just as I felt the night before visiting GiGi's grave. The jolt was painless; however, it did knock me down off of my knees and straight onto the floor. I did not understand what was happening to me. I never lost consciousness.

Everyone in the room began praying their separate prayers in a whisper of a voice. I managed to get back into a kneeling position. Feeling humble, I continued to pray out loud. And this is when I'm sure the journey of my old life ended and the resurrection of my new life began. I began crying, uncontrollably. I didn't know if some of the sadness had to do with fear or that the old Rachel was gone.

The cardinal, Retsis, Michael, and Daniel made a circle around me where I knelt. They joined hands and continued to pray. I continued to feel small jolts of electricity shooting through my body. All fear was gone. I knew that I was going to be fine. As their prayer's became louder and louder, Cardinal Jessepe sprinkled holy water on me. Michael and Retsis were praying in Italian, Daniel and Gabriel in English. They prayed for my faith to remain unbroken and for my strength to increase along with knowledge. I kept my eyes closed the entire time of prayer.

The noise of thunder from the sky clapped loudly; the room that we were in vibrated. The outside thunder and rain seemed to validate the presence of our Almighty God. The prayers ceased, and I opened my tearful eyes. Cardinal Jessepe reached his hand out to help me up from my knees to my feet. The thunder had stopped, and so did the rain. Silence filled the room. I looked around and Daniel, Gabriel and Michael were gone. Retsis and two nuns were at my side, as I stood to my feet with the help of the Cardinal.

"Where is Michael, Gabriel, and Daniel?" I asked.

Retsis held me tight and said, "They went to see a friend in the hospital who has been in a coma for some years now. They visit this friend every week to make sure that her physical body is functioning properly. It simply isn't her time yet."

"Where is this friend at right now?"

Retsis said, "In a rehabilitation hospital right here in New York."

"If you don't mind me asking, Retsis, how did their friend end up in a coma?"

Retsis responded, "She was hit by a speeding car some years ago and never regained consciousness. However, from what I've heard and seen, the doctors and nurses caring for her say that her physical body has been in tip top shape for the past eight years until recently. Last week her heart went into some sort of heart malfunction, and the doctors had to defibrillate her heart to keep her from dying."

I continued to ask Retsis questions. "That is awful. What happened to their friend, what is their friend's name and how old is she?" At that point, Retsis didn't respond because Cardinal Jessepe cut her off.

The cardinal said, "Rachel, if you don't mind, Retsis, Sister Anne and Sister Margaret are going to remain with you here for the next twenty one days."

Sister Margaret, a middle-aged woman held a wet towel in her hand waiting for the right time to wipe my forehead.

"Are you feeling OK, Rachel?" Sister Anne asked. "You look pale and tired."

"She will be fine, Sister Anne," Sister Margaret responded.

"Yes, I'm OK, Sister Anne. I feel tired and a bit faint, but I'm sure after a good nights rest that I'll be just fine in the morning," I said.

Sister Anne assisted me across the room into a comfortable chair, where Sister Margaret wiped my face with the cool cloth. Sister Margaret's affections toward me were mother like and nurturing. I needed all of the attention that I could get at this point in my life.

Retsis and the cardinal were talking at the other end of the room. I couldn't hear what they were saying from where I was sitting. The cardinal walked toward me with Retsis following.

"Rachel, you will remain here in this holy sanctuary for the next twenty one days where you will fast as needed, pray, and learn everything that there is to know about national and international affairs," he said.

Sister Margaret walked away for a brief moment and returned with a cold glass of orange juice. I was most certainly thirsty. I drank the juice fast without interruption. I looked over at the cardinal and said, "I am ready."

The cardinal began to speak as the two sisters and Retsis stood right beside me listening. "This is what we know thus far. There will be an attempted assassination on the pope's life. That four hundred and forty four people will be at risk of being murdered within eight years time. The president of the United States is at high risk for having a heart attack. The facts have been established that you will prevent these atrocities from happening. When you see the white dove and he flaps his wings three times your vessel, the one that you have entered into this world with, will enhance and your mission will begin. Your timing will not be the same, your outlook on life will be different, and all of the pieces like a puzzle will fall into place. There are no written instructions for you. You have been given twenty-one days to prepare, and that is all. There are no extensions on the time that you will remain here counting tomorrow as day number one. Rachel, you have had a long eventful day. Sister Margaret and Sister Anne will show you to your room."

I thanked the cardinal for his hospitality and said good night.

The two nuns escorted me up one flight of stairs and down a long corridor. At the end of the corridor on the right hand side, there was a door. Sister Margaret opened the door. The inside of the room was a lot larger than my room on campus. There was no television, no radio. One large bed, as well as a large bureau and mirror, filled the room. It was perfect for me. I also noticed that I had a private bathroom with no adjoining rooms. I thanked Sister Ann and Sister Margaret for showing me to my room and said good night. I was so tired that I could not think straight. I took off my clothes and stepped into the shower. Allowing the water to get as hot as possible, I stood underneath letting the water hit the top of my head. Everything that I needed was in this bathroom: towels washcloths, soap, and body lotion.

Someone had brought my clothes up to this room prior to my arrival. Quickly drying off with the towel around me, I reached inside my small bag pulled out my nightgown and bedroom slippers. I pulled the blankets back on the bed, laid down on the bed and looked up at the ceiling. I had reached the point of exhaustion, and my mind refuse to allow me to enter the realm of sleep. I looked out of the window up at the sky; I could see daybreak peeking through. For the first time ever, I was able to visualize heaven and the miracles of life on a spiritual side.

I thought about how my life would change again twenty- one days from now. Acceptance had begun its process within me, as evidenced by a drastic decrease in fear. An abundance of peace took over, allowing me finally to drift off to sleep.

I woke up just a few hours later to a knock at my bedroom door. It was Retsis, carrying three newspapers in her hand: A national newspaper, an international newspaper, and a local newspaper. How did Retsis look so refreshed after turning in during the wee hours this morning?

She entered the room and said, "Good morning, Rachel. How did you sleep last night?"

Still feeling a bit groggy from sleep deprivation, I responded, "Just fine, Retsis." I climbed back into bed. Retsis placed the three newspapers on the night table next to my bed.

"Rachel, for the next twenty days, I will bring you these newspapers, and I would strongly suggest you read every one of them everyday."

For the second time, I could see the physical resemblance that we had that would confirm, we were twins. Not identical but perhaps, fraternal twins.

"What are you doing awake so early, Retsis?"

"My dear Rachel, it isn't early. It is one o' clock in the afternoon."

I jumped out of bed. "Are you serious?"

"Of course I'm serious. Would you like brunch, Rachel?"

"Why yes, I'm starving."

"I'll have a tray sent up to you right away," she said.

I yelled out thanks while brushing my teeth in the bathroom.

After getting dressed and having breakfast, I decided to put my personal belongings away into the drawers. While opening one of the drawers, I noticed a large gray book with a picture of a white dove on the front. There was no title, no author's name. The book was filled with pictures, bright colorful pictures of people. Some of the photographs of people looked familiar to me. My curiosity had been struck. I sat at the edge of my bed quickly turning the pages.

I came to a page that had a picture of a young girl in a hospital. There were nurses and doctors around her bed. The photograph did not show the young girl's face. The reason I knew that this girl was young was because of her hands. Her hands were small and resembled the hands of a child. Next to this young girl sat an older woman in a chair next to the child's bed. It was apparent that this woman was engulfed with grief. She sat with her face in her hands. It appeared as if she were crying. Who was this woman? It had to have been the sick child's mother. I turned to the next page of the book, and I saw a picture of a white dove flying into the sunset. When I reached page four hundred and forty four there was a picture of this same young girl standing with her back facing the photograph. Again there were nurses and doctors standing around this girl along with men in suits holding cameras. The older woman sitting in the chair next to the girl's bed in this photograph was now standing in front of this young girl embracing her. I still could not see either of their faces. The last fifty pages of the book were blank.

I placed the book back into the drawer where I found it. I really did not know what to make of the pictures in that book. What I didn't understand was where were the words in the book? There was no written story to go with the pictures. Without wasting anymore time in this day, I picked up the international newspaper to read first. It really didn't matter to me which newspaper I read first because by the end of the day, all three had to be read.

CHAPTER
FIFTEEN

For the next four days straight, all I did was read newspaper articles. Sister Margaret and Sister Anne had brought my meals to me on a tray. That was the only time that I would stop reading, to eat. They made sure that I ate every meal. Everyday that passed by, I felt as if I was getting physically weaker and weaker. My appetite had increased, and I didn't know where this decrease in strength was coming from. I thought maybe it was because Retsis wasn't around.

I had not seen Retsis in about two days. When I inquired about where she had gone, Sister Anne said that she had joined Daniel, Gabriel, and Michael with visiting their sick friend.

I was truly grateful to have a group of friends who were so loyal. I didn't know anything about this girl who they were visiting, but one thing that I knew was that she was a lucky person to have them looking after her. Although I didn't know who she was, my heart went out to her family.

Family, that was something that I have longed for as far back as I can remember. GiGi rarely spoke about any family members. As far as I knew, GiGi was the only child. Monty, my mother, was the only child. And my grandfather, GiGi's husband, was the only child. This validated my status as an orphan for sure. The good news was that I had Retsis. The sad news was worrying how long she would be allowed to walk with me through life. I have accepted that she is my sister, my guardian angel, and definitely my source of strength. When she is away and not directly in my presence, I feel as if someone literally blew the light out to my soul. To fathom any part of my life without her is incomprehensible.

I had been in this room for six days reading. This meant that all I had left was fifteen days to set a plan in motion. Was I supposed to have a plan? Or was everything just supposed to fall in place as the cardinal said? I had not left this room for seven days, and I was starting to get a case of cabin fever.

Everything that I needed was right here in this convent. The nuns were helpful with locating any material related to current events that I requested, and so was Retsis when she was around. Sister Anne came to my room to inform me that Mass was scheduled to begin at 7 a.m.

I was looking forward to attending Mass. This would allow me to see the cardinal again, and perhaps Daniel, Gabriel, and Michael. I knew for sure that Retsis would attend tomorrow's Mass. Sister Anne gave me a briefing on what to expect; after all, I was a Baptist. Excitement had set in, and I began looking through the closet for my best dress. I had none. Sister Margaret knocked on the door. When she entered into the room she had a beautiful robe in her hand.

"What is that, Sister Margaret?" I said.

"This is a robe made specially for you to wear tomorrow."

"The colors are beautiful, Sister Margaret. Why did you go through so much trouble making that robe for me?" She handed me the robe and the material felt like a soft crepe cotton blend. The green gold and dark purple print was soothing to the eyes.

"Oh my dear child, it was no trouble at all. Besides, the cardinal would like for you to wear this holy robe not only tomorrow, but also for the next two Sundays after tomorrow. Please try this head wrap on for me, Rachel, so that I may make last minute adjustments if necessary."

"I would love to. I'll try on the robe also. If that is all right with you"

"Of course its all right, my child."

I went into the bathroom and tried the robe and headpiece on. I resembled an African Princess from the Congo. Sister Margaret gasped as I walked out of the bathroom in this beautiful attire. My hair that was sticking out of the sides of the headpiece, Sister Margaret pulled it back tight and fastened with a hair clamp that she pulled out of the pocket of her black robe. While looking in the mirror, she put her face to mine and said, "You my darling could pass for my daughter. What a remarkable resemblance you have to me."

I smiled and said, "Thank you Sister. I'll take that as a compliment."

Sister Margaret was beautiful. Olive-colored skin with deep setting almond black eyes. Her hair was dark brown and naturally curly. I didn't want to take the gown off. I looked simply magnificent. I looked in the mirror one last time and took the gown and head piece off. Sister Margaret left with the gown in her hand.

"With some minor adjustments, Rachel, it will be perfect. Rachel, you know everyone cannot wear this gown. There have been only two others before you to wear one like it." I really did not want to ask who the two were. I had enough surprises already.

"They were worthy to wear it," Sister Margaret said.

"Well, Sister Margaret, that makes me feel quite special," I said.

"You are special my dear child."

Sister Margaret left the room with my gown over her arm and said that she would return tonight with all of the adjustments made. I was excited and could not wait for morning to put the gown on to wear in public. All of those colors looked wonderful against my olive-colored skin. I too have dark brown, large almond shaped eyes. My high cheekbones often made me wonder if I had Indian blood flowing through my veins. With a last name of Legna, maybe I had some Italian or Spanish blood, too.

Time was rapidly passing by that evening, and that was great for me. Finally two hours later, Sister Margaret returned with the altered robe and headpiece in hand.

"Here Rachel, try this on now."

I went into the bathroom and put the robe back on along with the headpiece. It was a perfect fit. Sister Margaret's face lit up like a Christmas tree when I walked out of the bathroom fully robed.

"Rachel, you are now ready," Sister Margaret said.

"Ready for what?" I aid.

"For whatever you need to be ready for my child. I will come by in the morning at 7 a.m. to show you where the sanctuary is located."

"That would be great because this place is huge, and I know I'll get lost."

"Goodnight, Rachel. Can I get you a snack before I turn in for the night?"

"No thank you, Sister Margaret. I'm not hungry. I am ready to turn in for the night."

I gave Sister Margaret a hug, and thanked her once again for everything. I set my alarm clock for 6 a.m. Tomorrow I had also planned on fasting and praying. I was sure I would feel a lot stronger after that.

After taking a shower, I climbed in the bed, said my prayers, and fell off into a deep sleep. I awakened to the sound of voices. I looked over at my clock and it was 3:40 a.m. Who would be awake at this hour? The voices that I was hearing I could not make out any of the conversation. None of the voices were familiar to me. I decided to go and inspect what was going on. I put my bathrobe on and walked out into the corridor outside of my bedroom. The voices were coming from down the long hall. As I walked closer and closer to this room, I could hear a man say, "If we go beyond the twenty- first day, it will kill her."

Sister Margaret walked up behind me and tapped me on the shoulder. Needless to say she scared the daylights out of me. "What are you doing out of bed, Rachel, and what are you doing at this end of the hall at this hour?" she said.

"I awakened to voices got up to inspect where they were coming from, and here I am."

"Shhh! You must never go into this room right here, is that understood Rachel?"

"Yes, it's understood, Sister Margaret. I apologize if I'm out of line here."

"Let me escort you back to your room."

As soon as I got back to my room, I went back to bed. Before stepping into the bed, I felt that jolt of lightning go through my body just as it did the night before my visit to New York. There was no pain involved. My body fell to the floor, and I couldn't move. I was fully awake, but could not control the situation that I was in. While on the floor, I felt a second jolt of electricity that sent my body off of the floor by about two inches. I could not scream, and I could not move. Something told me not to fight this. It was obvious, that this strong force of energy was something that I could not control. After lying on the floor and unable to move for about five minutes, I regained some control of body movement. I bent my knees and stood to my feet. I climbed into bed and began to cry. I was afraid that I was dying. There was something seriously wrong with my physical health. Feeling weak and lightheaded, I managed to just doze off to sleep. Anticipating seeing Retsis at church service, I knew that she would know what I should do. If perhaps I could live until morning, things would get better.

I awakened early the next morning because I was anxious to get to early Mass to hear Cardinal Jessepe preach and to see Daniel, Gabriel, Michael, and Retsis. Perhaps they could give me a little more insight into where my life was at, and where I was supposed to be at as far as completing my scheduled task. More confusion had set in after finding that big gray book with the white dove on the front in the drawer the other day. I was sure that this book had something to do with the outcome of my life.

After taking a quick shower, I got dressed. After pulling my hair back away from my face just as Sister Margaret did, I placed the head piece on my head first, and then I put the multi-colored robe on. The robe and headpiece looked beautiful on me. The fit was perfect. Surely I was going to turn heads when I walked into the chapel downstairs.

Moments later I heard a knock at my bedroom door. I opened the door and there stood Gabriel, Daniel, Michael, and Retsis.

"It's so good to see you, Rachel," Daniel said.

Michael gave me his usual tight embrace.

"How are you hanging in there Rachel?" said Gabriel.

"I'm hanging in there, you guys. Come on inside. There are a couple of concerns that I have right now, one being my health. It started about two weeks ago. Every now and then I get this jolt of electrical energy that knocks me a couple of inches out of my space. It's painless; however, during these episodes, I have no physical control of my body. I am unable to call for help. It frightens me. Last night the electrical jolts hit me twice, it's obvious they are increasing with time. After these occurrences I have no energy and can barely move my body. What's happening to me? Am I dying?"

The three of my friends along with my sister, Retsis, looked at each other. Retsis began to speak. "My dear sister, some things we are just not supposed to know ahead of time. This much I can share with you—you are not going to die anytime soon. If you were going to die, you would have been dead eight years ago. When I speak of death, my sister, I speak of it in the flesh. There is eternal life for those who have earned it. Death does not exist in our world. Now please do not ask us anymore questions pertaining to the subject matter of death. That information is not privy for us to disclose. If immortals knew their time of death, their life would be impossible to live."

I smiled and said, "Yeah, you are right, Retsis. I agree."

"Rachel you must never leave this room without someone to escort you around these premises. This church is large with many doors that automatically lock behind you. We cannot take the chance of you getting lost here," Daniel said.

"I understand, Daniel. I guess Sister Margaret must have told you that she found me walking about last night."

"Yes, Rachel, she did," he said.

"I promise that will never happen again."

"We have a sermon to attend," said Michael.

"By the way, Rachel, you look like a guardian angel with that robe on," Gabriel said.

"Thank you, Gabriel. Sister Margaret made it for me. And I was grateful that she did. I had no decent dress in my possession for this occasion."

CHAPTER
SIXTEEN

Entering the cathedral was breathtaking. The ceiling inside the cathedral was high. There weren't many people sitting in the pews. The church was only half filled. Candles were lit everywhere. The music the organist was playing set the mood for any guardian or archangels welcoming. Daniel led the way into the cathedral, while the rest of us followed. We sat in the front of the church in the first pew.

Cardinal Jessepe appeared out of nowhere. He looked worn and tired in the face. He looked at me and acknowledged my presence with a nod of his head. I returned the nod with a smile. And he began his sermon.

As the cardinal spoke, chills went up my spine as he preached a sermon on Lazarus raising from the dead and the analogy of spiritual death and the resurrection of life. I was totally taken aback because I had heard this same sermon somewhere else. After thinking back in retrospect on my life, I realized that Pastor Neil, had preached this exact sermon word for word at GiGi's funeral. I sat listening as it took me back in time. As I thought back in time, I was thinking about situations that I had never experienced. I could see GiGi on her knees, not in her prayer closet, but in a room kneeling over a young child. GiGi is crying and asking someone to spare this child's life. GiGi appears to be sad. Getting up from her knees, GiGi gives this young girl who is lying in bed a kiss on the cheek and whispers into her ear, "I love you, Rachel." This never happened in the past. I was never sick. My mind was racing. I thought, what is happening to me, am I losing my mind? I screamed and ran out of the church up the back stairs in which I came down from my room.

Retsis ran behind me back to my room. "Rachel, what is wrong with you?"

"I don't know, Sister. I think I'm losing my mind. I just had some kind of a premonition. I saw GiGi leaning over me crying. GiGi is dead, and I have never witnessed GiGi ever crying over my bed."

"Rachel, what you need is a nice warm glass of milk and a nap. You haven't been getting much sleep lately, and we both know how the mind can play tricks on us when we're exhausted."

"Yes, you are right, I am exhausted. A nap will be great right now."

"I am going to leave you here now alone so that you can rest. I will return after Mass to look in on you."

I climbed into bed and fell into a deep sleep. I slept through until the next day. My body really needed that sleep. Since I arrived here, I had been functioning on four and five hours of sleep. Finally,

I felt like my old self and I was full of energy, and ready to go. This sleep pattern of eight hours per night was a regular pattern for me. Everything was back to normal here and quiet.

My normal schedule here I had resumed, reading every newspaper as I was told.

Seven more days had passed. I received three newspapers delivered to my room every morning. I needed to know everything that was going on in the world: from the hijacking of flight 487 on June 7, to the hostage take down in Georgia by the federal enforcement agency on June 11. It was apparent that the United States of America had its share of problems. On June 18, headlines of the *National Tribune* read, "President of the United States Dead at 42 Massive Heart Attack," and the headline and story were packaged with a large photograph of the vice president of the United States being sworn in to office.

Over the last two weeks, I had read many national and international articles to help prepare me for my political quest. All of this reading was something new for me. My knowledge of political information had increased ten fold. I knew what was going on all over the world, not just in America. While attending Yale, I was required to read many novels and textbooks, but reading so many different articles on current events was a new experience for me.

Out of all of the national and international headlines that I had read the headline that captured my attention the most was an article written June 17, about a seven-year-old girl who was struck by a moving vehicle. The article read, "It has been eight years since America's sleeping girl has been in a coma. The doctors are amazed how her physical body remains in tact after having had to defibrillate her small heart back into a normal rhythm on three occasions. Her grandmother continues to visit everyday. Never losing hope that her sleeping granddaughter will come out of her coma and smile for her again."

This sounded like Daniel, Gabriel, and Michael's friend who Retsis said had been in a coma. That poor girl so young, lying so helpless in a coma. My heart went out to her grandmother. Surely I would never have wanted GiGi to have to experience such a heartwrenching ordeal. As the newspapers were delivered to my room every morning along with my breakfast, I continued to read everything. Following the story of America's sleeping girl in a coma really struck my curiosity.

I opened that drawer where I had found that big gray book with the white dove on the front, and it was still there. I removed the book from the drawer and opened the book. Someone had added ten additional pages of pictures. The last time that I opened the book, the last page was four hundred and forty four. Now there were four hundred and fifty four pages. Sister Margaret was in the next set of photos. Sister Margaret was embracing this same young girl as if the girl were leaving. The young girl's back was facing the camera. Sister Margaret was crying. The only words that appeared in this book were under Sister Margaret's photo of her and this young girl. And it read: "My daughter you were taken away from me once. Returned only for me to have to give you up again. My heart is broken."

I continued to look at the pictures as I turned the pages. For some reason I could not bring myself to look at the last page in this book. I closed the book and put it back into the drawer. Perhaps tomorrow I would have the courage to view the last page. Just as I closed the drawer, there was a knock at my door.

"Come in," I yelled. It was Sister Margaret. "What a pleasant surprise. I was just thinking about you, Sister Margaret."

"I hope you don't mind me barging in on you. I was away for a few days visiting my daughter. When I returned, I heard that you were feeling a bit under the weather," she said.

"Oh yes, it was just that I was exhausted and run down."

"You must not allow your body to get run down, Rachel. You have just four days left here with us. We've grown fond of you. And when you return to your home, you must be healthy. You have a large job with much responsibility upon your return. By the way, I heard that you looked beautiful, Rachel, in that robe that I made for you. "

"Yes, I received many compliments. By the way, I didn't know that you had a daughter, forgive me but aren't you a nun?"

"No my dear child. I am not a nun. Although I have been living here in this rectory for the last fifteen years permitted by the highest authority, I am not a nun. My daughter is the young girl that you have seen in the pictures of the book. She is the same girl who Daniel, Gabriel, and Michael visit routinely. She has been gravely ill."

"I'm sorry to hear that, Sister Margaret. Is your daughter in a coma?"

"Yes, she is the girl that you have read about in the newspapers."

"Oh my! I'm sorry. Yes, I have been following that story. That must be your mother that the newspapers refer to when they say "America's sleeping girl's grandmother never loses hope that her granddaughter will one day come out of the coma and smile for her again.""

"Rachel, you are sharp. Yes, that is my mother who is at my daughter's bedside everyday all day. I am also there quite often. With other obligations and commitments, my time with my daughter has been limited."

"Where is your husband, the girl's father? If you don't mind me asking."

"My child, somethings are better left unmentioned."

"I understand. I'm sorry for being nosy."

"My child you owe me no apology. Now I must go. I will come back to see you right before you leave." Sister Margaret pulled my hair back off of my face before leaving as she often did, and gave me a kiss on the forehead.

"Thanks for stopping in, Sister Margaret. I'll see you again right before I leave."

"Oh Rachel, by the way, don't feel afraid to look at all of the pages in the book in the drawer. It will bring you closer to your curiosity."

How did Sister Margaret know that I was afraid to look at the last page in that book? How in this world did she know that I was looking in the book at all did I mention it to her? Maybe I did.

I am going to truly miss Sister Margaret when I leave here. There is just something so special about her that I adore. Since I have four days remaining here, I am going to surprise Retsis and Sister Margaret and show up in the dining room for dinner. Dinner is always served at 5 p.m. With ten minutes to find my way to the dining room, I had better leave now if I were going to spend adequate time dining.

Before leaving my room, I knew that finding the dining room in this huge cathedral would most definitely be a challenge. The long corridors with many doors and stairwells reminded me of a maze. Somehow I knew that any stairwell going down would leave me close to the dining room, which was on the main level. As I walked down the spiral staircase I could not help notice the many pictures on the walls of the stairwell.

Pictures of Daniel, Gabriel, and Michael were the only pictures that stood out for me, until I walked further down the stairwell. To my surprise, a large picture of Sister Margaret when she was younger and standing next to her was a picture of my GiGi. In the picture Sister Margaret was dressed in a plaid skirt with knee socks and had a book bag flung over her shoulder. How could this be? I thought. This was odd. Sister Margaret never mentioned to me that she knew my GiGi.

Reaching the bottom of the stairwell, I heard voices from a distance and smelled the fragrance of food. Following the sound of the voices and the smell of the food, I was standing at the doorway of the dining room. There sat, Retsis, Sister Margaret, Sister Anne, Daniel, Gabriel, and Michael. They were talking and laughing and when Retsis noticed me standing in the doorway, she cleared her throat and said, "Oh Rachel, come on in. We were not expecting you to join us."

Sister Margaret along with Gabriel and Daniel stood up and simultaneously said,

"What a pleasant surprise."

"With just four days left here to spend with all of you, I felt the need to see you all tonight," I said.

"Here come and sit next to me and fill up your plate. Dinner has just started, and we are delighted that you came down to join us," said Michael.

"It is a wonder that you found your way without getting lost," said Sister Margaret.

I sat down and began filling my plate with all of the goodies that was before me. I was famished. Fish, salad, rice, beets and many pies. Responding to Sister Margaret's question.

"How did you know that I didn't get lost, Sister Margaret?"

"Simply because if you had gotten lost, my dear child, you would not be sitting here with us at this table so soon. I just left you in your room fifteen minutes ago."

"Relax mother, it seems as if everyone is so uptight that Rachel didn't have an escort to bring her to the dining room. She is not a baby for crying out loud, she is fifteen years old," said Retsis.

I smiled at Sister Margaret and said, "You're right, and why is Retsis calling you mother, Sister Margaret? I beg your pardon, fifteen?"

"Yes, fifteen Rachel. For the first seven years of your life you knew nothing about nothing. Twenty two minus seven is fifteen," Retsis said.

Sister Anne's face had turned beet red from embarrassment of this conversation.

By this time everyone was silent. Sister Margaret answered, "My dear child, everyone calls me mother, and if you would like to call me mother I would be elated."

"How about if I just called you Monty?" I said.

"Well Rachel, if that would make you happy, then please, call me Monty. I have been called that also in the past."

Gabriel began coughing and coughing. Michael handed him a glass of water to drink.

As Gabriel gulped down the water quickly, I decided to speak from my heart. It was now or never.

"I just want you all to know that you all have brought much joy into my life. I was under the impression my entire life that I had no family and this experience has made that much better. For the first time in my life since my grandmother passed on, I have never felt such a sense of belonging and love. I'm not sure where my old life ended and my new life began, but what I am sure of is that just as I sit here before you, I know that when I leave here my heart tells me that I will probably never see any of you again. Whatever it is that I am supposed to do, what I ask of you is that you continue to guide my life in the direction I am supposed to go. As my guardian angels never leave my side, and please give me a sign so that I will know that you are near."

Retsis hugged me and said, "You are a part of me. We entered this world at the same time, and although I had to take on a different form and a different route I have never left your side. When you are sitting alone thinking of me, you will feel a small breeze and then you will know that I am near."

I began crying and ran back to the hallway. "Let her go," said Daniel, "She needs to be alone right now."

I cried myself to sleep. The sadness of not seeing my best friend and sister, Retsis, anymore was too much for me to bear. Without her, I could not have gotten through GiGi's death. How could I return to Yale without her?

CHAPTER
SEVENTEEN

The next morning, I had no appetite and I was overtaken by grief. To stay in bed was my choice for the day. However, I knew that was not an option. With three days left at this cathedral, the current events of the world were my first priority. Believe it or not, I was able to conjure up the strength to read the newspaper articles before me for the day. June 25, eighteen days had gone by with three more left. The only exciting article was the one on the front page of the local *Tribune,* featuring a large photograph of the beautiful Saint Anthony's Cathedral on 108th Street and Madison Avenue. Now I knew where I was living. Since my arrival, I had not left this building and had no clue of the address. The headline read: "The Oldest Cathedral in New York City to Undergo Reconstruction." What caught my attention was that the cardinal standing in front of the church was not Cardinal Jessepe. The article named the cardinal as O'Brady. Where was Cardinal Jessepe The last time that I saw Cardinal Jessepe was at Mass last week. Nothing made sense to me anymore. And I decided that I was not going to try and make sense out of the impossible. Maybe with in the remaining three days there would be something in the newspaper that would direct me to the exit of my journey here. Thus far, nothing had given me any clues to why I was here.

I wrote down the date and event of all of the articles that provoked my curiosity or had a major impression on the world. I was not sure if I would need to refer to them in the future; my instincts told me that I would.

I felt that if I never left here perhaps that would be fine with me to spend the remainder of my life within the confines of these safe walls. What I needed was to relax my mind. Everything was moving too fast. Making a to-do list might put everything in perspective. My thoughts rolled in like fog on a rainy morning. Nothing was clear to me.

I did not know where I was going when I left here. How I was suppose to begin my mission, and who would be there waiting for me Daniel or Gabriel?

After this, my life would never be the same. Packing my clothes seemed to relieve some of the stress I was experiencing. My body seemed as if it was going through some physical changes, and I was getting weaker as the days went by. Compared to when I first arrived, the change was significant. I was tired all of the time. My endurance was limited, and I was getting the bolts of electricity through my body more frequently, and left me helpless. It had become difficult for me to stand for short periods of time. My legs would get weak, and I would quickly lose my balance.

The next two days had come and gone, and my anxiety was at an all-time high. Sister Margaret kept her promise and visited me the day before I was to leave. After entering my room, I could see that she had been crying. There was something wrong with Sister Margaret's demeanor.

"Sister Margaret, I can see that something is troubling you," I said, standing up out of my chair with great effort.

"Yes, my dear child," she said.

"Is it your daughter?"

"Yes, my dear child. It seems as if I am going to lose her again."

"Oh my! I'm so sorry. I'm so sorry. I wish that I could stay longer to help you get through this," I said, wobbling on my unsteady legs.

"Rachel, there is nothing that you can do. Thank you anyway for your concern," she said.

"If perhaps there is anyway that I can return, Sister Margaret, I will come back to visit. Perhaps your daughter won't die after all, you never know. You must have faith that those doctors are going to do everything in their power to keep her alive as long as she is in that hospital."

"I know, and I do have faith, Rachel. I guess I'm just grieving for something that I never had," she said.

"Think of the situation in a positive light, Sister Margaret. Your daughter has been in a coma for eight years now. Maybe her physical body is tired, and she needs to go to another place."

Sister Margaret kissed me on the forehead, gave me a tight hug, said good-bye, and made me promise her that I would never forget her until we met again. I reluctantly made her the promise, not knowing if I could make good of it. As she left my room she was crying and didn't turn back around to look at me as she left.

Retsis had arrived with Michael to say their good-byes. Why

were they coming to say good-bye so soon? I was not supposed to leave until tomorrow.

"Hello, Rachel, we thought that we would come to say our good-byes today instead of tomorrow. You might need to gather your thoughts and pack your belongings tomorrow," Michael said.

"I'm already packed, and it would take me longer than tomorrow to gather all of my thoughts. Am I going to get the opportunity to see Daniel and Gabriel before leaving?" I said.

"Rachel, they sent a message with us to give to you. They apologize for not being able to say good-bye in person. They had to go to the bedside of our friend who is in a coma. She has taken a turn in her condition, and the next twenty four hours is going to be touch and go," Michael said.

"Rachel, my sister, I am going to miss you. Remember what I told you. When you think of me and feel that cool breeze pass your body, you'll know that I am there with you," Retsis said, while giving me the warmest hug.

"I will never forget you all. My life won't be the same without you. And when I blink my eyes twice when you're around, know that I am responding to your presence and that I feel the breeze. I love you, Michael. I love you, Retsis. Good-bye."

They both left the room at the same time. Just as fast as they entered my life, they were gone. What was all of this about? The cardinal said that when the time came, I would know what to do in order to save the lives of the four hundred and forty four people. I still felt as blind to my journey as when I left Yale. I had absolutely no idea of the master's plan, yet. Once again, I cried myself to sleep out of frustration of not knowing what to do and the sorrow of knowing I would be alone without Retsis and Michael.

Awakening early to the sound of a bird flapping its wings, I looked out of the window, and on the window ledge, I couldn't help notice a big white beautiful dove flying into the sky.

At that second, I felt a jolt of painless electricity go through my body. All went silent and dark. "I'm dying," I said to no one.

CHAPTER
EIGHTEEN

"Doctor, doctor. She's opening her eyes."

"Not likely after eight years," I heared the doctor say.

"This is a miracle, come over here doctor. You need to see this for yourself. She is asking for someone by the name of Retsis," said the nurse as she stood over me with a stethoscope in her hand.

I took a deep breath after feeling like my lungs were deprived of air. My mouth was dry, and my body felt as if pins were underneath the mattress sticking me. Total discomfort from head to toe would best describe what I was feeling. Attempting to lift my arm, I could feel someone holding down my hand. I tried to turn my head to the side. GiGi whimpered in a chair next to my bed. The tears were rolling down her face, just as I had seen in the large book of photos at the cathedral. I couldn't talk. How did GiGi come back from the dead? Was this a bad dream? The effort of staying awake was too much for me. I fell back off to sleep. I could hear GiGi giving permission to the photographers to take photographs. Flashes of light awakened me as photographers snapped photographs. Doctors and nurses were everywhere. GiGi still sat at my bedside. This time after awakening I was able to whisper to GiGi.

"What happened to me, GiGi?" I said.

Tears once again rolled down her face.

"Rachel, eight years ago you were playing with a ball in the street and a speeding car hit you. Ever since then, September 30, 1955, you were in a coma," GiGi said, in a whisper.

"What day is it GiGi?" I asked.

"Today is January 24,1963," GiGi said.

"How old am I, GiGi?"

"You just had a birthday three months ago. You are now fifteen years old. You were seven years old, a month from turning eight, when you were hit by that car."

"Fifteen, that is impossible."

"Rachel, try and get some rest. You need to take it easy right now," GiGi said.

"One more question, GiGi. Where am I?"

"You are at Saint Anthony's convalescent home. The nuns along with the doctors and nurses have done a wonderful job in keeping you alive," GiGi said.

"Why am I dressed in this beautiful robe, while in bed? The colors are magnificent the texture feels like a crepe silky material."

"An old woman who visited you every week since you have been in the coma dropped it off. Her name is Anne. She insisted, on me having the nurses put this robe on you today. She called it her good-bye gift to you. I'm sorry that you will not get the opportunity to meet her. Anne had to leave town for good to take care of her ill sister. I'm sure she would be thrilled to know that finally our prayers were answered," GiGi said.

"My God, I never left."

"What did you say, Rachel?" GiGi said.

"Nothing, GiGi. I need a few minutes to gather my thoughts. This is a bit much for me to handle right now."

"I want you to take it easy, Rachel. Your body has been through a traumatic experience. The doctors had to shock your heart three times last month to get it to beat the right way. We almost lost you. All of my prayers have been answered."

"It's like an insurance policy, right GiGi?" I asked.

"You are exactly right. It's just like an insurance policy you keep praying and praying until it pays off."

"Miss Legna can you tell us how you are feeling right now after being in a coma for eight years?" the news reporter asked.

"Miss Legna is not up for visitors right now. Thank you," said my doctor.

"What about you, Mrs.Gallo? Can you give us a statement on how you never gave up on the fact that your granddaughter, America's sleeping girl, would smile for you again," said the reporter.

"I have no comments right now. I want to spend some quiet time with my granddaughter if you don't mind," GiGi said.

"I'm going to have to ask all of you reporters and photographers to leave here right now. I'm sure that Rachel Legna will be more than happy to answer all of your questions in the near future," the doctor with a blue name plaque identifying him as Dr. Harris.

Dr. Harris proceeded to examine me from head to toe. After answering an extensive amount of questions regarding my health, the doctor seemed surprised about some of the results of my physical assessment.

My blood pressure was normal. The sound of my heart was normal, and I no longer had an irregular rhythm, he said. I was able to move all of my extremities without any limitations while in bed. And I was ready to get out of bed. The doctor felt that it was too soon for me to get out of bed alone. He called for a physical therapist to help me to learn how to walk all over again. I had a swallowing evaluation done to make sure that I would not aspirate or choke to death while eating. If the results were good, that would mean that in time this stomach tube would come out and this ugly hole in my stomach would possibly heal.

CHAPTER
NINETEEN

GiGi was at my bedside everyday helping me to adjust to being awake. It was so good to have her around again that I almost forgot that I had remembered her dying three days before my sixteenth birthday in my dream. How could that have been a dream? When one is in a coma, I didn't think having dreams were possible. If it wasn't a dream, what was it? It suddenly hit me. The entire time that I was in a coma my life had continued. Could this be possible? I knew there was only one way to find out. I had to get well enough to leave this room. Or at least have access to a telephone to communicate outside of this room. I didn't want to ask GiGi for any favors, for she appeared exhausted. The black circles around her eyes were heavy.

"GiGi, why don't you go home and get some sleep? You look

exhausted," I said.

"Maybe I'll take you up on that offer sweetie," GiGi said.

"GiGi, do we still live on 23rd street?" I asked.

"We sure do sweetie, and I still pray in my little closet everyday before coming up here to visit with you," GiGi said.

I smiled and gave GiGi a kiss "I think that is wonderful, GiGi. On your way out, could you send someone in to give me an update on my condition?" I said.

"Absolutely my sweetie," GiGi said.

GiGi left and about five minutes later a nun came into the room. She was fairly young about 45 years old.

"How can I help you, Rachel? The doctor is talking to your grandmother."

"Well, I was wondering if you could be so kind to answer some questions for me. What is your name?" I asked.

"My name is Sister Helen," she said.

"Sister Helen, can you tell me who the present cardinal is?"

"Why certainly, his name is O'Brady," the nun said.

"Is this cathedral getting ready to undergo reconstruction?" I asked.

"Why yes, Rachel. Did your grandmother tell you about it?" she said.

"No. Is this church located on One Hundred and Eigth Street and Madison Avenue?"

"Why yes, it is."

"My God, this cannot be. I need access to a telephone as soon as possible. How soon can I get out of here? " I asked the nun, while attempting to get out of bed.

The nun began yelling out for help. I was out of control and could not contain myself. I needed to get out of bed. Two doctors and a nurse entered my room.

"What's all the commotion about in here?" Dr. Harris asked.

"Doctor, she became upset after I answered a couple of questions that she had asked me. She became upset attempting to get out of bed," the nun said.

"Doctor, I need to get out of this bed to walk around this church. I need to see the entire third and fourth floors along with the dining room in the basement," I said.

"This is remarkable. How did you know that this church had three levels, and that the dining room was on the lower level? Did your grandmother mention it to you?" Dr. Harris asked while the others looked on intently.

"No! Neither did she mention to me that there was a set of spiral stairs leading directly to the dining room on the lower level of this cathedral," I said.

"Did Miss Gallo leave yet? Can someone check?" Dr. Harris asked.

The nurse ran out of my room, only to return a minute later.

"She just left doctor," the nurse said.

"Someone give her a call at her apartment in about a half hour, please. We need to ask Mrs. Gallo a few questions regarding her past conversations with her granddaughter. If Mrs. Gallo had not had these conversations with Rachel, I think that we may have something remarkable here," said the doctor.

"If I can get someone to help me to walk, I can find my old room," I said.

"Rachel, try and remember as much as you can about situations that you think that might have occurred while you were in a coma," said Dr. Harris.

"Doctor, I have one question for you. Is it possible for someone to dream while in a coma?"

"Rachel, nothing suprises me anymore, and yes, anything is

possible. Perhaps, some events are accepted by the medical community; however, I've seen situations in my practice that have been unexplainable. Therefore, I am opened to receive the impossible. What I can tell you about being in a coma is that you are in a state of unconsciousness. There is no awareness and no conscious control of anything. It's getting late, and you need your rest. We will contact your grandmother as soon as she gets home OK" Dr. Harris said.

Dr. Harris left the room along with the nurse, the nun and the other doctor. I could hear some of the conversation continued outside of my room where they were standing.

"What a medical phenomenon it would be if her life had continued while she was in a coma," I said.

I also heard him say that I was extremely intelligent for fifteen year old. And my analytical abilities were beyond any fifteen year old that he had ever come in contact with.

Regardless of what level of intelligence I was at, nothing could explain what I was about to encounter next. It had been six months since I awakened from my coma. Every day was a challenge for me to get back to the level of physical function prior to my accident and to maintain my sanity after realizing that I was the vessel of a supernatural experience. I had to keep every aspect of my life in perspective. After all it had been confirmed that GiGi had never mentioned anything to me about the location of any part of this building or the renovations expected to begin next month. Everyone here knew that something out of the ordinary happened to me after being struck by that car.

Never to fall in harms way again, I had found the beautiful rock in the nightstand next to my bed. This was the same small rock that had been given to me by Michael. I kept it in my pocket never to walk without it. I was cautious not to squeeze it tight for I feared that I would have a relapse, remembering how it had sapped my energy in the past. I had no energy to gamble with at that point in my life. As the days past, I would remember certain situations that occurred when I was in the coma.

Different images of people and events surfaced in my mind. As the days went by, my physical health progressed. I was now able to walk around with the use of a walker and without anyone's assistance. This meant more independence for me. Deep down inside, I knew that I had to get beyond the level of this floor where this room was located. This meant that I had to wait until the nuns turned in for the night. Until the day shift nurses gave report to the one nurse in charge at night, I wouldn't be able to maneuver my way off the floor without this walker and without letting anyone know—Not even GiGi, as she continued to visit faithfully everyday.

It wasn't until her visit today that I was beside myself with memories that validated that I was given insight into the future. GiGi arrived at Saint Anthony's everyday to visit me. At noon we would have lunch together. Then I would nap while she read to me and she would leave after I awakened to complete my physical therapy.

CHAPTER
TWENTY

One day, GiGi decided to read from the book of Daniel as I stretched out on the bed. The tears began rolling down my face. When she mentioned the name Michael while reading from this book, I remembered Retsis, I remembered Gabriel, and I remembered Sister Margaret. I sat straight up in the bed.

"My God, GiGi. I remember," I said.

"Remember what, sweetie?"

"Tell me, GiGi. Did I have a twin sister who died at birth? Have you ever taken a picture with my mother with her wearing a plaid skirt, a navy blue sweater, white blouse with her book bag flung over her left shoulder? Was my mother's name Margaret? Who is the president of the United States?" I screamed out.

"Child slow down, before you have a heart attack. Yes," she said with hesitation, "You had a twin sister who died at birth along with your mother, Margaret." GiGi's eyes searched my face for a reaction. She had a look of uncertainty on her face. "Margaret died of complications moments after you were born, and the doctors could not save your sister. I thought I would also die that day, but I had to live to take care of you."

GiGi began crying. "How come you didn't tell me GiGi?" I said.

"Sweetie, I didn't think that you would understand. I didn't want to pile anymore guilt on you. When I told you how your mother died, you became withdrawn and I saw how the guilt cropped up in you. I just didn't think that it would make a difference if I didn't tell you," GiGi said.

She continued to answer my questions. " Yes! Your mother and I did take a picture and in the picture she was wearing exactly what you have described. The picture was taken when your mother was about your age. Last, but not least, the name of the president of the United States in his last term this year of the eight years served is President Gorden. Running for the presidency is Andrew Lewis, the youngest man ever to run for the presidency of the United States. He is 42 year old. His running mate is Seymour Johnson," GiGi said.

I said, "GiGi, please call my doctor in here. I have something that I need to tell all of you."

GiGi said, while wiping the tears away from her eyes, "It is obvious that something different happened to you, Rachel. Maybe you should not tell everyone right now."

I said, "GiGi, I know that you have been through a rough time with this entire ordeal not knowing if I was going to live or die."

GiGi interrupted, "Yes, and I felt responsible for what happened to you because I allowed you to go downstairs and play alone without me watching you."

"I totally understand, GiGi, but please know that it wasn't your fault. This was supposed to happen to me. With the information that I have now, I realize that this was written before my time. No one could have stopped that dreadful accident. If it hadn't happened, I would not be able to say what I am about to say. And what I am about to say is going to save the lives of many," I said.

By the look on GiGi's face, I knew that she didn't agree with what I was saying.

GiGi said, "My sweetie, some things are better left unknown."

Giving GiGi a tight hug and kiss to comfort her, I said, "Yes, GiGi you're right. Somethings, but not all things are better left unknown."

GiGi looked at me, smiled, and said, "You are a replica of your mother. Not only do you behave like her with your persistent attitude, you look like her."

I said, "I know."

She pulled my hair back off of my face, just as Margaret had done through out my experience while in a coma. I gave GiGi the biggest smile my face could create. "Now GiGi, please go and get the doctor for me while I have these memories fresh in my mind," I said.

GiGi got up and left the room to get Dr Harris.

Moments later, Dr. Harris returned with GiGi and asked, "Rachel, your grandmother says that you are having some concerns that are really upsetting you right now. Is that true?"

I said, "Yes Dr. Harris, that is true, and these concerns I would like to discuss with you."

I could tell by Dr. Harris' facial expression that he was eager to hear what I was about to say. He pulled up a chair beside my bed. GiGi also sat in a chair next to my bed listening. And I began telling him the story of my life as I saw it through my eyes for the past fifteen years, beginning with the day I was hit by that speeding car.

"Dr. Harris, I hope you don't have other patients to visit for a while because this may take some time," I said. Dr. Harris didn't budge and motioned to me with his hand to continue.

"On September 30, 1955, GiGi sent me outside to play. I noticed a red ball in the corner of the doorway of our apartment building. I began bouncing the ball and the ball rolled out of my hands and into the street. At that exact same time, I heard a small voice call my name. In a whisper of a voice, 'Rachel.' I turned around, and there was a small girl who looked just like me. She said that her name was 'Sister.' Anyway, we proceeded to talk and when GiGi came downstairs, Sister was gone. It was like she vanished in thin air."

I continued on with my life with GiGi. The daily routine of living, going to school and the years went by without incident. I graduated from elementary school and went on to high school, where I met a girl named Retsis and a boy named Michael. The two of them were inseparable. I befriended Retsis and Michael, and we eventually became best friends."

Dr. Harris interrupted me while writing on a piece of paper, "Did you say that this girls name was Retsis?"

"Yes," I said.

"I have you to know, Rachel, that RETSIS is SISTER written backwards on paper," he said.

I shook my head and continued with my story. "As my friendship grew closer to Retsis we began planning a big sweet sixteen birthday party. And for the first time, Retsis was going to meet GiGi."

At this point I became emotional, and the tears rolled down my face as I continued to speak. "Three days before my sweet sixteenth birthday, GiGi passed away. Retsis was there to help me through this. As a matter of fact, Retsis was the one who found your insurance policy, GiGi, for one million dollars."

GiGi screamed. Dr. Harris got up out of his chair to console GiGi as she sat sobbing her eyes out.

"What is it, Mrs. Gallo?" Dr. Harris said.

"My God, I do have an insurance policy that I have been keeping from Rachel worth one million dollars. I wanted her to be well taken care of, considering we have no other family members alive. There is absolutely no way that Rachel could have known that doctor," GiGi said.

"Calm down Mrs. Gallo. I can understand why you're upset. This is surprising," Dr. Harris said.

"May I continue? Are you OK, GiGi?' I asked.

"Yes, sweetie. I'm fine." GiGi said.

Dr. Harris said, "Rachel, before I allow you to continue, I need to get the media in here. That is with your consent Mrs. Gallo."

"Sure you have my consent." GiGi said. Dr. Harris handed GiGi a piece of paper to sign. I imagined it was the consent form.

"This is something that has never happened here before. You may say something that will have an impact on the world. With what I have come up with this far after investigating your case, Rachel, I do not feel that I am putting my reputation on the line. There are certain things that you have mentioned to me since you have been here, such as where certain rooms are located in this church. Lets not waste any more time here," Dr. Harris said.

"I suggest you get them in here fast before I forget again," I said.

Dr. Harris quickly left the room to make a phone call, and to cancel the rest of his appointments for the day. When he returned he said, "Rachel, I just want you to know that whatever you say will be written down by these reporters and most likely be published in all newspapers all over the world. Do you understand that you don't have to tell us about this. Would you like her to have an attorney present, Mrs. Gallo?" Dr. Harris asked.

"I'm sure she is being represented as she speaks by the best," GiGi said.

By the expression on the doctor's face, I could tell that he thought that GiGi was crazy. He couldn't understand her concept of representation as being the representation of a higher authority.

"No, Dr. Harris. We do not need legal representation," GiGi said.

"You may perhaps want to get paid financially for this story. You know, Rachel, you can probably make a million dollars from this," Dr. Harris said.

"I'm sure I can Dr. Harris, but I decline. My soul is worth more than a million dollars," I said.

GiGi looked at me and smiled. That confirmed that my decision to tell my story for the love of mankind was not for sale.

"Rachel, your life will never be the same after you speak with the media," Dr. Harris said.

"Dr. Harris, my life changed permanently eight years ago your time and fifteen years ago my time. When I came out of this coma, I had completed two years of college at Yale. That's why my intellect is not one of a fifteen year old," I said.

Dr. Harris looked at me and smiled. "That makes more sense," he said.

By this time, the reporters had arrived in my room. The doctor began introducing me and GiGi to the reporters and giving them a general idea on why they were invited to Saint Anthony's.

"This is Rachel Legna. She is fifteen years old. Eight years ago

Rachel was struck by a speeding car as she played outside her apartment building on 23rd Street here in Manhattan. Since then, Rachel has been in a coma. She was admitted to St. Luke's Hospital, where after six months in a coma she was transferred here to Saint Anthony's, where she has been ever since. You all were invited here today because you have been following America's Sleeping Girl since she's been in a coma. And you all are aware that six months ago on January 23, 1963, she awakened from that coma and has been progressively recovering here since then. She has celebrated her fifteenth birthday with us, and in October of 1963 will turn sixteen. Since her awakening, Rachel has not left this facility. She has no telephone and has had no access to the outside except for her grandmother, who has been sitting at her bedside from the day of the tragedy. I will now turn over to you, Rachel Legna. Please allow Miss Legna the opportunity to finish her story before asking any questions. Thank you," Dr. Harris said.

CHAPTER
TWENTY-ONE

The reporters had cameras for photographs and notepads to write on.

"I will not begin telling you how I got here because you all know that. I am going to pick up my story where I left off with Dr. Harris earlier," I said.

"Three days from my sixteenth birthday, my grandmother was found dead in her little prayer closet the date October 16, 1963. I cashed in on her one million-dollar-insurance policy and went on with my life as GiGi would have wanted me to. With the help of my best friend Retsis, life wasn't as complicated as I anticipated. The both of us, Retsis and I graduated from high school. By this time, I had become close to a friend that I had met through Retsis named Michael. Michael was different, and so was Retsis. After high school, we decided that we would remain together as friends and attend the same college. In September 1964, we enrolled at Yale University under a full scholarship. For the next two years, our lives were inseparable until one night right before we were supposed to take a trip to Italy to visit the pope. Michael and Retsis revealed to me who they really were."

The reporters were snapping pictures and writing fast on their notepads.

I continued: "Retsis said that she was my twin sister who died at birth, and Michael said that he was my guardian angel. Needless to say, I was in shock. Professor Daniel and Professor Gabriel, who taught at Yale, said that the trip to Italy was canceled, and that we needed to get to New York right away. Upon arrival in New York, I was brought to a hugh cathedral and introduced to a Cardinal Cardonni Jessepe. This man proceeded to hint at my mission in life, without informing me exactly what the mission was, and, or how I was supposed to carry it out. I was confused. Professor Daniel and Professor Gabriel had asked that I no longer referred to them as professors but to call them by name only. I did. My life had began to really get strange. I was told by Retsis and the cardinal that I had to read every newspaper article that I could get my hands on, and that would shed some light to what I was supposed to accomplish. That's what I did for the twenty one days I resided at the cathedral."I stopped speaking and motioned for a glass of water.

"Are you OK, Rachel? Do you wish to continue?" Dr Harris said.

"Yes, I'm fine," I said.

"The cardinal informed me that I was supposed to save the lives of four hundred and forty four people. Meanwhile, after being at this cathedral for two weeks, I began feeling jolts of electrical energy bolt through my body, leaving me physically helpless. With a total of three occurances, I began getting weaker and weaker as the days went on. I thought I was dying. I wanted to see Gabriel and Daniel again, thinking that they could help, and I was told by Retsis that they were visiting a friend who was in a coma. I was introduced to Sister Margaret and Sister Anne who were nice to me. They lived at the rectory. Sister Margaret often visited this same young girl who was in a coma. She said the girl was her daughter. The night before I was due to leave this church, Sister Maragret was upset. She said that she was losing her daughter for the second time. I tried to console her, unsuccessfully. I managed to get a look at the dining room of this place, and I passed by a room that I was told by Sister Margaret to never walk the halls or go into any of the rooms. The room that I almost entered was this room."

The photographers and reporters were stunned. The breathing sounds they were making were loud. The reporters began talking loudly amongst each other respecting Dr. Harris' requests of no interruptions.

"Please, allow me to continue," I yelled. "I was told upon arrival to this cathedral by Cardinal Jessepe that after the twenty-first day when I saw the white dove flap its wings three times, my mission would begin. I saw a white dove flap its wings and fly off into the sky right before awakening from my coma. Now I will take your questions one by one, by a show of hands please."

In the small room without windows about twenty reporters had their hands raised. I chose randomly trying to give everyone a chance at a question. "Yes, you standing in the back, what is your question?" I asked.

"Miss Legna, I could not help notice that Retsis is Sister spelled backwards, and your last name Legna is Angel spelled backwards. What can you tell us about that?" the reporter said.

"Well, I had a twin sister who died at birth. My mother died at the same time. I believe Retsis was my twin Sister who died at birth. My last name as Angel spelled backwards, I was never aware of that. Next question, please," I said.

"You mentioned, Rachel, that you found your grandmother dead three days before your sixteenth birthday. You haven't turned sixteen yet, and what are your plans three days before your sixteenth birthday?" the reporter said.

"Well, sir, I'm not sure if I can change the future. But if I can prevent my grandmother from having a heart attack, most certainly I will try. Three days from my sixteenth birthday my grandmother is going to be in a hospital hooked up to a cardiac monitor and all precautions will be taken to prevent her death. Next question," I said.

"Rachel, you said that you attended two years at Yale. Is there any additional information that you can provide us with that could validate your presence there within the last eight years?" the reporter asked.

"What you must realize is that I was given insight into the future. Seven years into the future. I have no knowledge of Yale today; however, I can tell you that within the next seven years there will be a fast food resturaunt on the south end campus of Yale called Maximillion's. I can also tell you that I can give you information on the course of my studies that would validate my major in biochemistry and theology in which I later transferred my major to," I said.

"Would you give us a little information that you picked up at Yale?" he said.

"Sure," I said. I began explaining the components of the human anatomy—all of the electrolytes and their functions pertaining to the human body. I explained the intra and extracellular exchange of potassium and sodium. I recited the periodic table of chemical components from left to right until I reached the bottom. "You guys, I was almost eight years old when I was hit by that car. Test me and you will find that my I.Q. is not of an eight year old but of an adult. Also, if you all would like you can take a trip to Yale to see if there is a small photograph of Abraham Lincoln's mother Nancy Hanks on the wall of the library at Shepard Hall. I was told by Retsis that it had been hanging on that wall since the 1962. Next question please." I said.

One reporter yelled out, "How do we know that you haven't read that somewhere in a book?"

"I was seven years old when my life was put on hold for eight years. I can assure you at seven years old that I had no interest in books of that nature. I had just learned how to read. This knowledge would have been well over my head. I was in a coma since 1955," I said.

"Rachel, during this journey you mentioned that you had to read newspaper articles. Can you tell us some of the articles you read?" the first reporter said.

"Yes, and I'm happy that someone finally asked that question. Some of the headlines that stand out in my mind are: June 18, 1971, 'President of the United States Dead at the Age of Forty nine. Massive Heart Attack.' "

I could hear someone in the back of the room say, "My God, if President Lewis gets elected in January during his last term he will be forty nine years old."

This triggered a frenzy with the press. I continued to tell the reporters about the articles of events I could remember. I continued: "June 7, 1971, 'Flight 487 to Scotland High Jacked, Four Passengers Murdered by Two Gunmen.' December 3, 1964, 'Thirty six people die in the Bombing of the Courthouse on Lafayette Street in Manhattan.' "

A reporter shouted, "Can you give us some information that would occur perhaps in the near future?"

I had to take a moment to think. The room was silent. By this time, there were more people in the room, including a psychologist and a psychiatrist.

"Yes, while attending Yale I completed a paper on 'The Hostage Takedown in Georgia' which occurred July 4, 1963, which is next week. Therefore you guys have no time to waste. Get on it. Two gunmen will enter an elementary school wearing masks. They will enter the school from the northeast emergency exit. Their objective is to have three of their leaders released from our prisons here in America. If this does happen, sixty children will be slaughtered," I said.

I looked over at GiGi and she was smiling and mumbling something under her breath while shaking her head in disbelief. I was exhausted.

Dr. Harris stepped up in front of now a crowd of about twenty people. "We will have to continue this conference at a later date Miss Legna is tired now. Please remember she is still in the recovery stage of her illness," he said.

"When will Rachel be able to go home Dr. Harris?" said a reporter.

"That is totally up to Miss Legna. She can stay as long as she'd like. We would love to bring her on board with our staff, after she finishes high school,"

Dr. Harris said.

"No offense, Dr. Harris, but I have no plans on attending high school. I will sit for a test and perhaps begin college again immediately after," I said.

Everyone in the room began laughing. The reporters shook my hand as they left my room. I felt relieved. I knew somewhere in the back of my mind that I had more information stored somewhere in my head. And this information was also vital to the world. I had finished poking around in my head for one day. I needed to rest. GiGi stayed with me the entire night. The nurses and nuns had found a cot in one of the other rooms and brought it to my room for GiGi to sleep on. I watched GiGi while she slept soundly. It was wonderful having her back in my life. I wanted to keep her in my life. I had to get out of Saint Anthony's before I turned sixteen.

There would be no birthday party, turning sixteen twice in one lifetime was enough for me. The frustration of being treated like a fifteen-year old was exhausting. I was given a second chance with life, only to have to repeat fourteen years of it over again. If I could get back to that room upstairs, maybe I could get some answers on how to make everything right again.

CHAPTER
TWENTY-TWO

September 30, 1980

Seventeen years ago at Saint Anthony's made a difference in many lives. The information that I had given had indeed saved lives. The F.B.I. was able to intercede in the hostage attempt in Georgia. No one was hurt and the two men responsible for the planning of the hostage attempt were captured and taken into custody. On December 3, 1964, there was a bombing of the courthouse on Lafayette Street in Manhattan. Fortunately, the building had been evacuated due to anticipation of the bombing, and no one was hurt. President Lewis was elected president of the United States. He refused medical attention during his first three years in office and died of a massive heart attack in his fourth year. On June 7, 1971, the hijacking of Flight 487 to Scotland never took place. The F.B.I. was able to intercede once again, saving the four passengers who might have died at the hands of the terrorists. The men planning this attempt were taken into custody. The gunman at Times Square ended up commiting suicide when approached by undercover agents right before getting on the elevator to approach the rooftop, where he had planned on slaughtering sixty six innocent pedestrians below. Last, but not least, grandmother died two days prior my eighteenth birthday. I would like to believe that the two extra years given to her was a gift of life on my behalf. She died from a massive heart attack. Fortunately, this time I was with her at her time of death. She died in my arms while whispering, "I love you, Rachel." I donated the money from her insurance policy to charity because I knew I would never get the opportunity to spend it.

When it was all said and done, I had indeed saved the lives of four hundred and forty four people just as Cardinal Jessepe prophesied. I completed college with a degree in theology at Saint Anthony's School of Seminary. Yale was not the university of my choice. I had attended Yale and could not imagine repeating the same courses without Retsis and Michael.

I stayed on here at Saint Anthony's, working as a counselor to those who needed counseling and made a big difference for the better in the many lives I touched. I loved it. I even counseled a man who approached me in the form of Natasto. I felt nothing, no attraction to him. For I knew it was the last trick of the enemy to keep me from rejoicing in the end. I sent him on his way. He would never cross my path again.

Scholars had come from all over the world to study my coma experiences, and no one was able to come up with a rationale of how and why this all came about. Cardinal Jessepe was appointed the cardinal after Cardinal O'Brady died in 1968. Our initial introduction by Sister Helen was ironic. Both of us knew that we had already met before this day of shaking hands. Cardinal Jessepe smiled at me whispered in my ear, "It is good to see you again, Rachel."

I returned the smile while shaking my head not in disbelief but in amazement asking the cardinal, "How is everyone?" Everyone meaning Monty, Retsis Michael, Daniel, Gabriel, Sister Anne, and GiGi.

Cardinal Jessepe answered in a whisper, "They are all with you."

The tears rolled down my face, and I retired to my room. The same room in which I occupied for the twenty one days of preparation for my return to this life. I sat at the edge of the bed opened up the book with the dove on the front cover, and all of the pages were there. I guess this meant that my life was now complete. Placing the book back into the drawer I knew that my purpose in life was at full circle. An abundance of sadness filled the room. I was going to miss this place. And at that moment I felt a strong breeze. Without a doubt, I knew that Retsis, Monty, Michael, and GiGi were here. I blinked my eyes twice as I had promised them I would in the past, or should I say in the future, to confirm my knowledge of their presence. I lied down on my bed took a deep breath and, closed my eyes, for my work was finished here. No more, returning to this world. That small stone that I carried with me had disappeared from my pocket. I didn't need it anymore. It was my time to exit gracefully into the arms of my master. I was ready after thirty three years. No one had to inform me of where I was going because I knew. Within seconds, I was with my entire family on the other side. And the experience was beautiful. From the beginning of time I was supposed to be here on earth. It was twenty-five years to the day when Retsis and I first met. And that's what it was all about— saving the four hundred and forty four lives including my own.